She really was fragile, Hugo thought, bending down to give his niece a hug. Last year had been a tragedy for Ruby, and it still showed. She expected calamity.

'This isn't ruin,' he said gently. 'It's just flour.'

'It's snow. To make Polly feel better when we're not here.'

'And Polly loves it,' Polly said, and then sneezed as if she needed to accentuate the point. 'Ruby, it's still great. Look what we've done, Dr Denver. All we need you to do is chop down a tree, so I suggest you stop dripping and start helping while I clean up your mess…'

'*My* mess?'

'Your mess,' she said, and grinned. 'Walking in on artists at work…you should know better.'

'I'm glad I didn't,' he said faintly, and he looked around at the mess and thought for the first time in…how long?…that this place looked like home.

What was better than this? he thought. What was better than Polly?

Dear Reader,

I was raised in a farming community, where everyone knew everyone and where our doctor seemed the linchpin of our lives. Doc—he needed no other name—was known to walk fifteen miles between clinics during wartime petrol rationing. By the time he delivered me he was in his eighties, and he worked on until I was in my teens. We never called him unless we truly needed him, but when we did he gave his all. I remember his grandson telling me what it was like at Doc's house at Christmas. You couldn't move for whisky, he said, and grateful gifts of home-baked goodies and produce were almost an embarrassment. When he died, the entire district mourned.

In a way, this book is a testament to Doc and to the caring community I was raised in. My husband and I have recently—joyously—moved back to a small town. As I write this I'm looking forward to Christmas in our new/old home, in our new/old community, and I'm wishing you the magic of belonging. I'm also wishing you the love shown by Doc, and by so many medical staff who follow his tradition of care, and I'm wishing you a very happy Christmas.

Marion Lennox

FROM CHRISTMAS TO FOREVER?

BY
MARION LENNOX

MILLS
BOON

First published in Great Britain 2015
by Mills & Boon, an imprint of Harlequin (UK) Limited,
Eton House, 18-24 Paradise Road, Richmond, Surrey, TW9 1SR

© 2015 Marion Lennox

ISBN: 978-0-263-26062-5

Printed and bound in Great Britain
by CPI Antony Rowe, Chippenham, Wiltshire

Marion Lennox is a country girl, born on an Australian dairy farm. She moved on, because the cows just weren't interested in her stories! Married to a 'very special doctor', she has also written under the name Trisha David. She's now stepped back from her 'other' career, teaching statistics. Finally she's figured out what's important, and has discovered the joys of baths, romance and chocolate. Preferably all at the same time! Marion is an international award-winning author.

Books by Marion Lennox

Mills & Boon Medical Romance

The Surgeon's Doorstep Baby
Miracle on Kaimotu Island
Gold Coast Angels: A Doctor's Redemption
Waves of Temptation
A Secret Shared...
Meant-to-Be Family

Mills & Boon Cherish

A Bride for the Maverick Millionaire
Sparks Fly with the Billionaire
Christmas at the Castle
Nine Months to Change His Life
Christmas Where They Belong

Visit the Author Profile page
at millsandboon.co.uk for more titles.

To the many people
who've already made us welcome in our new home.
To Jacky, to Gail, to Colleen, to Alison,
and to all on Fisherman's Flat, to all who welcome us
as we walk our dog, paddle our kayaks,
or simply yak over the front fence.
You're stuck with us for life, and we love it.

CHAPTER ONE

CHRISTMAS IN THE middle of nowhere. Wombat Valley. *Hooray!*

Dr Pollyanna Hargreaves—Polly to everyone but her mother—beefed up the radio as she turned off the main road. Bing Crosby's 'White Christmas' wasn't exactly appropriate for Christmas deep in the Australian bush, but it didn't stop her singing along. She might be a long way from snow, but she was happy.

The country around her was wild and mountainous. The twisting road meant this last section of the journey could take a while, but the further she went, the further she got from the whole over-the-top celebration that was her parents' idea of Christmas.

'You can't be serious!' She could still hear her mother's appalled words when she'd broken the news that she wouldn't be spending Christmas with them. 'We've planned one of the most wonderful Christmases ever. We've hired the most prestigious restaurant on Sydney Harbour. All our closest friends are coming, and the head chef himself has promised to oversee a diabetic menu. Pollyanna, everyone expects you.'

Expectation was the whole problem, Polly thought, as she turned through the next curve with care. This road was little more than a logging route, and recent rain had gouged gutters along the unsealed verge. The whole of New South Wales had been inundated with weeks of subtropical downpours, and it looked as if Wombat Valley had borne the brunt of them. She was down to a snail's pace.

But she wasn't worried. She wasn't in Sydney. Or in Monaco, where she'd been last Christmas. Or in Aspen, where she'd been the Christmas before that.

Cute little Pollyanna had finally cut and run.

'And I'm not going back,' she told the road ahead. Enough. She felt as if she'd been her parents' plaything since birth, saddled with a preposterous name, with nannies to take care of every whim and loaded with the expectation that she be the perfect daughter.

For Polly was the only child of Olivia and Charles Hargreaves. Heiress to the Hargreaves millions. She was courted and fussed over, wrapped in cotton wool and expected to be...

'Perfect.' She abandoned Bing and said the word aloud, thinking of the tears, the recriminations, the gentle but incessant blackmail.

'Polly, you'll break your mother's heart.' That was what her father had said when Polly had decided, aged seven, that she liked chocolate ice cream, eating a family tub behind her nanny's back and putting her blood sugars through the roof. And ever since... 'You know we worry. Don't you care?'

And then, when she'd decided she wanted to be a doctor...

'Pollyanna, how can you stress your body with a demanding career like medicine? Plus you have your inheritance to consider. If you need to work—which you don't—then at least take a position in the family company. You could be our PR assistant; that's safe. Medicine! Polly, you'll break our hearts.'

And now this. Breaking up with the boy they wanted her to marry, followed by Not Coming Home For Christmas. Not being there to be fussed over, prettied, shown off to their friends. This was heartbreak upon heartbreak upon heartbreak.

'But I'm over it,' she said out loud. 'I'm over families—over, over, over. I'm an independent career woman so it's time I started acting like one. This is a good start. I'm five hours' drive from Sydney, in the middle of nowhere. I'm contracted to act as locum for two weeks. I can't get further away than this.'

And it was exciting. She'd trained and worked in city hospitals. She didn't have a clue about bush medicine, but the doctor she was relieving—Dr Hugo Denver—had told her things would be straightforward.

'We're usually busy,' he'd said in their phone interview. 'The valley could use two doctors or more, but over Christmas half the population seems to depart for Sydney or the coast. We run a ten-bed hospital but anything major gets helicoptered out. Mostly we deal with minor stuff where it's not worth the expense of sending for the Air Ambulance, or long-termers, or locals who choose to die in the Valley rather than in acute city hospitals.'

'You provide palliative care?' she'd asked, astonished.

'Via home visits, mostly,' he'd told her. 'Most of our oldies only go to the city under duress, and it's an honour to look after them at home. I also deal with trauma, but the logging industry closes down for three weeks over Christmas and the place is quiet. I doubt if you'll have much excitement.'

'But I wouldn't mind a bit of excitement,' she said aloud as she manoeuvred her little sports car around the next bend. 'Just enough to keep me occupied.'

And then, as if in answer to her prayers, she rounded the next bend—and got more excitement than she'd bargained for.

Dr Hugo Denver was well over excitement. Hugo was cramped inside a truck balanced almost vertically over the side of a cliff. He was trying to stop Horace Fry from bleeding out. He was also trying not to think that Ruby was totally dependent on him, and his life seemed to be balanced on one very unstable, very young tree.

The call had come in twenty minutes ago. Margaret Fry,

wife of the said Horace, had managed to crawl out of the crashed truck and ring him.

'Doc, you gotta come fast.' She'd sobbed into the phone. 'Horace's bleeding like a stuck pig and there's no one here but me.'

'He's still in the truck?'

'Steering wheel jabbed him. Blood's making him feel faint.'

'Bleeding from where?'

'Shoulder, I think.'

'Can you put pressure on it?'

'Doc, I can't.' It was a wail. 'You know blood makes me throw up and I'm not getting back in that truck. Doc, come, fast!'

What choice did he have? What choice did he ever have? If there was trauma in Wombat Valley, Hugo was it.

'Ring the police,' he snapped. 'I'm on my way.'

Lois, his housekeeper, had been preparing lunch. She'd been humming Christmas carols, almost vibrating with excitement. As was Ruby. As soon as the locum arrived they were off, Lois to her son's place in Melbourne, Hugo and Ruby to their long-awaited two-week holiday.

Christmas at the beach... This was what his sister had promised Ruby last year, but last year's Christmas had become a blur of shock and sorrow. A car crash the week before. A single car accident. Suicide?

Hugo's life had changed immeasurably in that moment, as had Ruby's.

Twelve months on, they were doing their best. He was doing his best. He'd moved back to Wombat Valley so Ruby could stay in her home, and he fully intended to give her the longed-for beach Christmas.

But commitment meant committing not only to Ruby but to the community he lived in. The locals cared for Ruby. He cared for the locals. That was the deal.

Lois had been putting cold meat and salad on the table.

She'd looked at him as he disconnected, and sighed and put his lunch in the fridge.

'Ring Donald,' he'd told her. Donald was a retired farmer who also owned a tow truck. It was a very small tow truck but the logging company with all its equipment was officially on holidays since yesterday. Donald's truck would be all the valley had. 'Tell him Horace Fry's truck's crashed at Blinder's Bend. Ring Joe at the hospital and tell him to expect casualties. Tell him I'll ring him as soon as I know details, and ask him to check that the police know. I need to go.'

'Aren't you expecting the new doctor?' Lois had practically glowered. She wanted to get away, too.

'If she arrives before I get back, you can give her my lunch,' he'd said dryly. 'I'll eat at the hospital.'

'Should I send her out to Blinder's? She could start straight away.'

'I can hardly throw her in at the deep end,' he'd told her. 'Hopefully, this will be the last casualty, though, and she'll have a nice quiet Christmas.' He'd dropped a kiss on his small niece's head. 'See you later, Ruby. Back soon.'

But now...

A quiet Christmas was just what he wanted, he thought grimly as he pushed hard on the gaping wound on Horace's shoulder. The steering wheel seemed to have snapped right off, and the steering column had jabbed into Horace's chest.

And he'd bled. Hugo had stared in dismay into the truck's cab, he'd looked at the angle the truck was leaning over the cliff, he'd looked at the amount of blood in the cabin and he'd made a call.

The truck was balanced on the edge of the cliff. The ground was sodden from recent rain but it had still looked stable enough to hold. He'd hoped...

He shouldn't have hoped. He should have waited for Donald with his tow truck, and for the police.

It didn't matter what he should have done. Margaret had been having hysterics, useless for help. Hopefully, Donald and his tow truck were on their way but he'd take a while. The police had to come from Willaura on the coast, and he hadn't been able to wait.

And then, as he'd bent into the cab, Horace had grasped his wrist with his good arm and tried to heave himself over to the passenger seat. He was a big man and he'd jerked with fear, shifting his weight to the middle of the cabin...

Hugo had felt the truck lurch and lurch again. He'd heard Margaret scream as the whole verge gave way and they were falling...

And then, blessedly, the truck seemed to catch on something. From this angle, all he could see holding them up was one twiggy sapling. His life depended on that sapling. There was still a drop under them that was long enough to give him nightmares.

But he didn't have time for nightmares. He'd been thrown around but somehow he was still applying pressure to Horace's arm. Somehow he'd pushed Horace back into the driver's seat, even if it was at a crazy angle.

'You move again and we'll both fall to the bottom of the cliff,' he told Horace and Horace subsided.

To say his life was flashing before his eyes would be an understatement.

Ruby. Seven years old.

He was all she had.

But he couldn't think of Ruby now. He needed to get back up to the road. Horace had lost too much blood. He needed fluids. He needed electrolytes. He needed the equipment to set up a drip...

Hugo moved a smidgen and the truck swayed again. He glanced out of the back window and saw they were ten feet down the cliff.

Trapped.

'Margaret?' he yelled. 'Margaret!'

There was no reply except sobbing.

His phone... Where the hell was his phone?

And then he remembered. He'd done a cursory check on Margaret. She'd been sobbing and shaking when he'd arrived. She was suffering from shock, he'd decided. It had been an instant diagnosis but it was all he'd had time for, so he'd put his jacket across her shoulders and run to the truck.

His phone was still in his jacket pocket.

'Margaret!' he yelled again, and the truck rocked again, and from up on the cliff Margaret's sobs grew louder.

Was she blocking her husband's need with her cries? Maybe she was. People had different ways of protecting themselves, and coming near a truck ten feet down a cliff, when the truck was threatening to fall another thirty, was possibly a bad idea.

Probably.

Definitely?

'That hurt!' Horace was groaning in pain.

'Sorry, mate, I need to push hard.'

'Not my shoulder, Doc—my eardrum.'

Great. All this and he'd be sued for perforating Horace's eardrum?

'Can you yell for Margaret? We need her help.'

'She won't answer,' Horace muttered. 'If she's having hysterics the only thing that'll stop her is ice water.'

Right.

'Then we need to sit really still until help arrives,' he told him, trying not to notice Horace's pallor, deciding not to check his blood pressure because there wasn't a thing he could do about it. 'The truck's unstable. We need to sit still until Donald arrives with his tow truck.'

'Then we'll be waiting a while,' Horace said without humour. 'Donald and his missus have gone to their daughter's for Christmas. Dunno who's got a tow truck round here. It'll have to be a tractor.'

'Can you get Margaret to ring someone?'

'Like I said, Doc, she's useless.'

* * *

There was an SUV parked right where she wanted to drive.

It was serviceable, dirty white, a four-wheel drive wagon with a neat red sign across the side. The sign said: 'Wombat Valley Medical Service'.

It blocked the road completely.

She put her foot on the brake and her car came to a well-behaved standstill.

The road curved behind the SUV, and as her car stopped she saw the collapse of the verge. And as she saw more, she gasped in horror.

There was a truck below the collapse. Over the cliff!

A few hundred yards back she'd passed a sign declaring this area to be Wombat Valley Gap. The Gap looked to be a magnificent wilderness area, stretching beneath the road as far as the eye could see.

The road was hewn into the side of the mountain. The edge was a steep drop. Very steep. Straight down.

The truck looked as if it had rounded the curve too fast. The skid marks suggested it had hit the cliff and spun across to the edge. The roadside looked as if it had given way.

The truck had slipped right over and was now balanced precariously about ten feet down the cliff, pointing downward. There were a couple of saplings holding it. Just.

A woman was crouched on the verge, weeping, and Polly herself almost wept in relief at the sight of her. She'd escaped from the truck then?

But then she thought... SUV blocking the road. Wombat Valley Medical Service... Two vehicles.

Where was the paramedic?

Was someone else in the truck? Was this dramas, plural? *Help!*

She was a city doctor, she thought frantically. She'd never been near the bush in her life. She'd never had to cope with a road accident. Yes, she'd cared for accident victims, but that had been in the organised efficiency of a city hospital Emergency Room.

All of a sudden she wanted to be back in Sydney. Preferably off-duty.

'You wanted to be a doctor,' she told herself, still taking time to assess the whole scene. Her lecturers in Emergency Medicine had drilled that into her, and somehow her training was coming back now. *'Don't jump in before you've checked the whole situation. Check fast but always check. You don't want to become work for another doctor. Work out priorities and keep yourself safe.'*

Keeping herself safe had never been a problem in the ER.

'You wanted to see medicine at its most basic,' she reminded herself as she figured out what must have happened. 'Here's your chance. Get out of the car and help.'

My, that truck looked unstable.

Keep yourself safe.

The woman was wailing.

Who was in the truck?

Deep breath.

She climbed out of her car, thinking a flouncy dress covered in red and white polka dots wasn't what she should be wearing right now. She was also wearing crimson sandals with kitten heels.

She hardly had time to change. She was a doctor and she was needed. Disregarding her entirely inappropriate wardrobe, she headed across to the crying woman. She was big-boned, buxom, wearing a crinoline frock and an electric-blue perm. She had a man's jacket over her shoulders. Her face was swollen from weeping and she had a scratch above one eye.

'Can you tell me what's happened?' Polly knelt beside her, and the woman stared at her and wailed louder. A lot louder.

But hysterics was something Pollyanna Hargreaves could deal with. Hysterics was Polly's mother's weapon of last resort and Polly had stopped responding to it from the age of six.

She knelt so her face was six inches from the woman's. She was forcing her to look at her and, as soon as she did, she got serious.

'Stop the noise or I'll slap you,' she said, loud and firm and cold as ice. Doctor threatening patient with physical violence... *Good one*, Polly thought. *That's the way to endear you to the locals*. But it couldn't matter. Were there people in that upside down truck?

'Who's in the truck?' she demanded. 'Take two deep breaths and talk.'

'I...my husband. And Doc...'

'Doc?'

'Doc Denver.'

'The doctor's in the truck?'

'He was trying to help Horace.' Somehow she was managing to speak. 'Horace was bleeding. But then the ground gave way and the truck slid and it's still wobbling and it's going to fall all the way down.'

The woman subsided as Polly once again took a moment to assess. The truck was definitely...wobbling. The saplings seemed to be the only thing holding it up. If even one of them gave way...

'Have you called for help?' she asked. The woman was clutching her phone.

'I called Doc...'

'The doctor who's here now?'

'Doc Denver, yes.'

'Good for you. How about the police? A tow truck?'

The woman shook her head, put her hands to her face and started loud, rapid breathing. Holly took a fast pulse check and diagnosed panic. There were other things she should exclude before a definitive diagnosis but, for now, triage said she needed to focus on the truck.

'I need you to concentrate on breathing,' she told the

woman. 'Count. One, two, three, four—in. One, two, three, four—out. Slow your breathing down. Will you do that?'

'I…yes…'

'Good woman.' But Polly had moved on. Truck. Cliff. Fall.

She edged forward, trying to see down the cliff, wary of the crumbling edge.

What was wrong with Christmas in Sydney? All at once she would have given her very best shoes to be there.

CHAPTER TWO

TRIAGE. ACTION. SOMEHOW POLLY made herself a plan.

First things first. She phoned the universal emergency number and the response came blessedly fast.

'Emergency services. Fire, ambulance, police—which service do you require?'

'How about all three?' She gave details but as she talked she stared down at the truck.

There was a coil of rope in the back of the truck. A big one. A girl could do lots with that rope, she thought. If she could clamber down…

A police sergeant came onto the phone, bluff but apologetic.

'We need to come from Willaura—we'll probably be half an hour. I'll get an ambulance there as soon as I can, but sorry, Doc, you're on your own for at least twenty minutes.'

He disconnected.

Twenty minutes. Half an hour.

The ground was soggy. If the saplings gave way…

She could still see the rope, ten feet down in the back of the truck tray. It wasn't a sheer drop but the angle was impossibly steep.

There were saplings beside the truck she could hold onto, if they were strong enough.

'Who's up there?'

The voice from the truck made her start. It was a voice she recognised from the calls she'd made organising this job. Dr Hugo Denver. Her employer.

'It's Dr Hargreaves, your new locum, and you promised

me no excitement,' she called back. She couldn't see him. 'Hello to you, too. I don't suppose there's any way you can jump from the cab and let it roll?'

'I have the driver in here. Multiple lacerations and a crush injury to the chest. I'm applying pressure to stop the bleeding.'

'You didn't think to pull him out first?'

There was a moment's pause, then a reply that sounded as if it came through gritted teeth. 'No.'

'That was hardly wise.'

'Are you in a position to judge?'

'I guess not.' She was assessing the saplings, seeing if she could figure out safe holds on the way down. 'But it does—in retrospect—seem to have been worth considering.'

She heard a choke that might even have been laughter. It helped, she thought. People thought medics had a black sense of humour but, in the worst kind of situations, humour was often the only way to alleviate tension.

'I'll ask for your advice when I need it,' he retorted and she tested a sapling for strength and thought maybe not.

'Advice is free,' she offered helpfully.

'Am I or am I not paying you?'

She almost managed a grin at that, except she couldn't get her sandals to grip in the mud and she was kind of distracted. 'I believe you are,' she said at last, and gave up on the shoes and tossed her kitten heels up onto the verge. Bare feet was bad but kitten heels were worse. She started inching down the slope, moving from sapling to sapling. If she could just reach that rope...

'I'd like a bit of respect,' Hugo Denver called and she held like a limpet to a particularly shaky sapling and tried to think about respect.

'It seems you're not in any position to ask for anything right now,' she managed. She was nearing the back of the truck but she was being super-cautious. If she slipped she could hardly grab the truck for support. It looked like one push and it'd fall…

Do not think of falling.

'I need my bag,' Hugo said. 'It's on the verge where the truck…'

'Yeah, I saw it.' It was above her. Quite a bit above her now.

'Can you lower it somehow?'

'In a minute. I'm getting a rope.'

'A rope?'

'There's one in the back of the truck. It looks really long and sturdy. Just what the doctor ordered.'

'You're climbing down?'

'I'm trying to.'

'Hell, Polly…'

'Don't worry. I have really grippy toenails and if I can reach it I might be able to make the truck more secure.'

There was a moment's silence. Then… 'Grippy toenails?'

'They're painted crimson.'

He didn't seem to hear the crimson bit. 'Polly, don't. It's too dangerous. There's a cord in my truck…'

'How long a cord?' Maybe she should have checked his truck.

'Twelve feet or so. You could use it to lower my bag. Horace needs a drip and fast.'

There was no way she could use a twelve-foot cord to secure the truck—and what use was a drip if the truck fell?

'Sorry,' Polly managed. 'In every single situation I've ever trained in, triage is sorting priorities, so that's what I've done. If I lower your bag and add a smidgen of weight to the truck, you may well be setting up a drip as you plummet to the valley floor. So it's rope first, secure the truck next and then I'll work on getting your bag. You get to be boss again when you get out of the truck.'

'You've got a mouth,' he said, sounding cautious—and also stunned.

'I'm bad at respect,' she admitted. If she could just get a firmer hold... 'That's the younger generation for you. You want to override me, Grandpa?'

'How old do you think I am?'

'You must be old if you think a ride to the bottom of the valley's an option.' And then she shut up because she had to let go of a sapling with one hand and hope the other held, and lean out and stretch and hope that her fingers could snag the rope...

And they did and she could have wept in relief but she didn't because she was concentrating on sliding the rope from the tray, an inch at a time, thinking that any sudden movements could mean...

Don't think what it could mean.

'You have red hair!'

He could see her. She'd been so intent she hadn't even looked at the window in the back of the truck. She braved a glance downward, and she saw him.

Okay, she conceded, this was no grandpa. The face looking out at her was lean and tanned and...worried. His face looked sort of chiselled, his eyes were deep set and his brow looked furrowed in concern...

All that she saw in the nanosecond she allowed herself before she went back to concentrating on freeing the rope. But weirdly it sort of...changed things.

Two seconds ago she'd been concentrating on saving two guys in a truck. Now one of them had a face. One of them looked worried. One of them looked...

Strong?

Immensely masculine?

How crazy was that? Her sight of him had been fleeting, a momentary impression, but there'd been something about the way he'd looked back at her...

Get on with the job, she told herself sharply. It was all very well getting the rope out of the truck. What was she going to do with it now she had it?

She had to concentrate on the rope. Not some male face. Not on the unknown Dr Denver.

The tray of the truck had a rail around it, with an upright at each corner. If she could loop the rope…

'Polly, wait for the cavalry,' Hugo demanded, and once again she had that impression of strength. And that he feared for her.

'The cavalry's arriving in half an hour,' she called back. 'Does Horace have half an hour?'

Silence.

'He's nicked a vein,' he said at last, and Polly thought: *That's that, then.* Horace needed help or he'd die.

She wedged herself against another sapling, hoping it could take her weight. Then she unwound her rope coil.

'What are you doing?' It was a sharp demand.

'Imagine I'm in Theatre,' she told him. 'Neurosurgeon fighting the odds. You're unscrubbed and useless. Would you ask for a commentary?'

'Is that another way of saying you don't have a plan?'

'Shut up and concentrate on Horace.' It was unnerving, to say the least, that he could see her, but then Horace groaned and Hugo's face disappeared from the back window and she could get on with…what…? Concentrating not on Hugo.

On one rope.

Somehow she got the middle of the rope looped and knotted around each side of the tray. Yay! Now she had to get back to the road. She clutched the cliff as if she were glued to it, scrambling up until her feet were on solid ground. Finally she was up. All she had to do now was figure out something to tie it to.

She had the shakes.

'Are you safe?' Hugo called and she realised he couldn't see her any more. The truck was too far over the lip. 'Dr Hargreaves?' There was no disguising his fear.

'I'm safe,' she called back and her voice wobbled and she

tried again. This time her voice was pleasingly smug. 'Feet on terra firma. Moving to stage two of the action plan.'

'I thought you didn't have a plan.'

'It's more exciting without one, but I'm trying. Indeed, I'm very trying.'

Plans took brains. Plans required the mush in her brain to turn useful. To stop thinking about Hugo plunging downward...

It wasn't Hugo. It was two guys in a truck. *Take the personal out of it*, she told herself.

Plan!

She needed a solid tree, or at least a good-sized stump. She had neither.

Attach the rope to her car? Not in a million years. Her little yellow sports car would sail over the cliff after the truck.

Margaret looked kind of buxom. How would she go as an anchor?

She gave a wry grin, wishing she could share the thought with Bossy In The Truck. Maybe not.

Bossy's truck?

The thought was no sooner in her mind than she was running up the road to Hugo's car. Blessedly, his keys were in the ignition. *Yes!* A minute later, his vehicle was parked as close as she could manage to the point where the truck had gone over.

It was an SUV. She'd once gone skiing in an upmarket version of one of these—her boyfriend's. Well, her ex-boyfriend, she conceded. They'd been snowed in and the tow truck had had to winch them out.

Polly had been interested in the process, or more interested than in listening to Marcus whinging, so she'd watched. There'd been an anchor point...

She ducked underneath. Yes! She had the ends of the rope fastened in a moment.

Maybe she could pull the truck up.

Maybe not. This wasn't a huge SUV.

'Polly...' From below Hugo's voice sounded desperate. 'What are you doing?'

'Being a Girl Guide,' she yelled back. 'Prepare to be stabilised.'

'How...?'

'Pure skill,' she yelled back. 'How's Horace?'

'Slipping.'

'Two minutes,' she yelled back, twisting the rope and racking her brain for a knot that could be used.

Reef Knot? Round Turn and Two Half Hitches? What about a Buntline Hitch? Yes! She almost beamed. Brown Owl would be proud.

She knotted and then cautiously shifted the SUV, reversing sideways against the cliff, taking up the last slack in the rope. Finally she cut the engine. She closed her eyes for a nanosecond and she allowed herself to breathe.

'Why don't you do something?' It was Margaret—of course it was Margaret—still crouched on the verge and screaming. 'My Horace's dying and all you do is...'

'Margaret, if you don't shut up I'll personally climb the cliff and slap you for Polly,' Hugo called up, and Polly thought: *Uh oh.* He must have heard her previous threat. Some introduction to his new employee. Medicine by force.

But at least he was backing her and the idea was strangely comforting—there were two doctors working instead of one.

'Let's get you somewhere more comfortable,' she told the woman. She had a jacket draped over her shoulders. 'Is this Doc Denver's jacket?'

'I...yes. His phone's in the pocket. It keeps ringing.'

You didn't think to answer it? she thought, but she didn't say it. What was the point now? But if Emergency Services were trying to verify their location...

'I want you to sit in Doc Denver's truck,' she told Margaret. 'If the phone rings, can you answer it and tell people where we are?'

'I don't...'

'We're depending on you, Margaret. All you have to do is sit in the car and answer the phone. Nothing else. Can you do that?'

'If you save Horace.'

'Deal.' She propelled her into the passenger seat of the SUV and there was a bonus. More ballast. With Margaret's extra, not insubstantial, weight, this vehicle was going nowhere.

'I think you're stable,' she yelled down the cliff, while she headed back to the verge for Hugo's bag. She flicked it open. Saline, adrenaline, painkilling drugs, all the paraphernalia she'd expect a country GP would carry. He must have put it down while he'd leaned into the truck, and then the road had given way.

How to get it to him?

'What do you mean, stable?' he called.

'I have nice strong ties attaching the truck tray to your SUV,' she called. 'The SUV's parked at right angles to you, with Margaret sitting in the passenger seat. It's going nowhere.'

'How did you tie…?'

'Girl Guiding 101,' she called back. 'You want to give me a raise on the strength of it?'

'Half my kingdom.'

'Half a country practice in Wombat Valley? Ha!'

'Yeah, you're right, it's a trap,' he called back. 'You know you'll never get away, but you walked in of your own accord, and I'm more than willing to share. I'll even include Priscilla Carlisle's bunions. They're a medical practice on their own.'

Astonishingly, she giggled.

This felt okay. She could hear undercurrents to his attempt at humour that she had no hope of understanding, but she was working hard, and in the truck Hugo would be working hard, too. The medical imperatives were still there, but the flavour of black humour was a comfort all on its own.

Medical imperatives. The bag was the next thing. Horace had suffered major blood loss. Everything Hugo needed was in that bag.

How to get the bag down?

Lower it? It'd catch on the undergrowth. Take it down herself? *Maybe.* The cab, though, was much lower than the tray. There were no solid saplings past the back of the tray.

She had Hugo's nylon cord. It was useless for abseiling—the nylon would slice her hands—but she didn't have to pull herself up. She could stay down there until the cavalry arrived.

Abseiling... A harness? *Nope.* The nylon would cut.

A seat? She'd learned to make a rope seat in Abseil Rescue.

Hmm.

'Tie the cord to the bag and toss it as close as you can,' Hugo called, and humour had given way to desperation. 'I can try and retrieve it.'

'What, lean out of the cabin? Have you seen the drop?'

'I'm trying not to see the drop but there's no choice.'

His voice cracked. It'd be killing him, she thought, watching Horace inch towards death with no way to help.

'Did you mention you have a kid? You're taking your kid to the beach for Christmas? Isn't that what this locum position is all about?'

'Yes, but...'

'Then you're going nowhere. Sit. Stay.'

There was a moment's silence, followed by a very strained response.

'Woof?'

She grinned. *Nice one.*

But she was no longer concentrating on the conversation. Her hands were fashioning a seat, three lines of cord, hooked together at the sides, with a triangle of cord at both sides to make it steady.

She could make a knot and she could let it out as she went...

Wow, she was dredging through the grey matter now. But it was possible, she conceded. She could tie the bag underneath her, find toeholds in the cliff, hopefully swing from sapling to sapling to steady her...

'Polly, if you're thinking of climbing...you can't.' Hugo's voice was deep and gravelly. There was strength there, she thought, but she also heard fear.

He was scared for her.

He didn't even know her.

He was concerned for a colleague, she thought, but, strangely, it felt more than that. It felt...warm. Strong.

Good.

Which was ridiculous. She knew nothing about this man, other than he wanted to take his kid to the beach for Christmas.

'Never say *can't* to a Hargreaves,' she managed to call back. 'You'll have my father to answer to.'

'I don't want to answer to your father if you're dead.'

'I'll write a note excusing you. Now shut up. I need to concentrate.'

'Polly...'

'Hold tight. I'm on my way.'

CHAPTER THREE

IT NEARLY KILLED HIM.

He could do nothing except apply pressure to Horace's shoulder and wait for rescue.

From a woman in a polka dot dress.

The sight of her from the truck's rear-view window had astounded him. Actually, the sight of anyone from the truck's rear-view mirror would have astounded him—this was an impossible place to reach—but that a woman...

No, that was sexist... That anyone, wearing a bare-shouldered dress with a halter neck tie, with flouncy auburn curls to her shoulders, with freckles...

Yeah, he'd even noticed the freckles.

And yes, he thought, he was being sexist or fashionist or whatever else he could think of being accused of right now, but he excused himself because what he wanted was a team of State Emergency Personnel with safety jackets and big boots organising a smooth transition to safety.

He was stuck with polka dots and freckles.

He should have asked for a photo when he'd organised the locum. He should never have...

Employed polka dots? Who was he kidding? If an applicant had a medical degree and was breathing he would have employed them. No one wanted to work in Wombat Valley.

No one but him and he was stuck here. Lured here for love of his little niece. Stuck here for ever.

Beside him, Horace was drifting in and out of consciousness. His blood pressure was dropping, his breathing was becoming laboured and there was nothing he could do.

He'd never felt so helpless.

Maybe he had. The night they'd rung and told him Grace had driven her car off the Gap.

Changing his life in an instant.

Why was he thinking about that now? Because there was nothing else to think about? Nothing to do?

The enforced idleness was killing him. He couldn't see up to the road unless he leaned out of the window. What was she doing?

What sort of a dumb name was Polly anyway? he thought tangentially. Whoever called a kid Pollyanna?

She'd sent a copy of her qualifications to him, with references. They'd been glowing, even if they'd been city based.

The name had put him off. Was that nameist?

Regardless, he'd had reservations about employing a city doctor in this place that required definite country skills, but Ruby deserved Christmas.

He deserved Christmas. Bondi Beach. Sydney. He'd had a life back there.

And now…his whole Christmas depended on a doctor in polka dots. More, his life depended on her. If her knots didn't hold…

'Hey!'

And she was just there, right by the driver's seat window. At least, her feet were there—bare!—and then her waist, and then there was a slither and a curse and her head appeared at the open window. She was carefully not touching the truck, using her feet on the cliff to push herself back.

'Hey,' she said again, breathlessly. 'How're you guys doing? Would you like a bag?'

And, amazingly, she hauled up his canvas holdall from under her.

Horace was slumped forward, semi-conscious, not re-acting to her presence. Polly gave Horace a long, assessing look and then turned her attention to him. He got the same glance. Until her assessment told her otherwise, it seemed he was the patient.

'Okay?' she asked.

'Bruises. Nothing more. I'm okay to work.'

He got a brisk nod, accepting his word, moving on. 'If you're planning on coping with childbirth or constipation, forget it,' she told him, lifting the bag through the open window towards him. 'I took stuff out to lighten the load. But this should have what you need.'

To say he was gobsmacked would be an understatement. She was acting like a doctor in a ward—calm, concise, using humour to deflect tension. She was hanging by some sort of harness—no, some sort of seat—at the end of a nylon cord. She was red-headed and freckled and polka-dotted, and she was cute...

She was a doctor, offering assistance.

He grabbed the bag so she could use her hands to steady herself and, as soon as he had it, her smile went to high beam. But her smile still encompassed a watchful eye on Horace. She was an emergency physician, he thought. ER work was a skill—communicating and reassuring terrified patients while assessing injuries at the same time. That was what she was doing. She knew the pressure he was under but her manner said this was just another day in the office.

'Those bruises,' she said. 'Any on the head? No concussion?'

So he was still a patient. 'No.'

'Promise?'

'Promise.'

'Then it's probably better if you work from inside the truck. If I work on Horace from outside I might put more pressure...'

'You've done enough.'

'I haven't but I don't want to bump the truck more than necessary. Yell if you need help but if you're fine to put in the drip then I'll tie myself to a sapling and watch. Margaret is up top, manning the phones, so it's my turn for a spot of R and R. It's time to strut your stuff, Dr Denver. Go.'

She pushed herself back from the truck and cocked a quizzical eyebrow—and he couldn't speak.

Time to strut his stuff? She was right, of course. He needed to stop staring at polka dots.

He needed to try and save Horace.

Polly was now just as stuck as the guys in the truck.

There was no way she could pull herself up the cliff again. She couldn't get purchase on the nylon without cutting herself. The cord had cut her hands while she'd lowered herself, but to get the bag to Hugo, to try and save Horace's life, she'd decided a bit of hand damage was worthwhile.

Getting up, though… Not so much. The cavalry was on its way. She'd done everything she could.

Now all she had to do was secure herself and watch Hugo work.

He couldn't do it.

He had all the equipment he needed. All he had to do was find a vein and insert a drip.

But Horace was a big man, his arms were fleshy and flaccid, and his blood pressure had dropped to dangerous levels. Even in normal circumstances it'd be tricky to find a vein.

Horace was bleeding from the arm nearest him. He had that pressure bound. The bleeding had slowed to a trickle, but he needed to use Horace's other arm for the drip.

It should be easy. All he needed to do was tug Horace's arm forward, locate the vein at the elbow and insert the drip.

But he was at the wrong angle and his hands shook. Something about crashing down a cliff, thinking he was going to hit the bottom? The vein he was trying for slid away under the needle.

'Want me to try?' Polly had tugged back from the truck,

cautious that she might inadvertently put weight on it, but she'd been watching.

'You can hardly operate while hanging on a rope,' he told her and she gave him a look of indignation.

'In case you hadn't noticed, I've rigged this up with a neat seat. So I'm not exactly hanging. If you're having trouble… I don't want to bump the truck but for Horace…maybe it's worth the risk.'

And she was right. Priority had to be that vein, but if he couldn't find it, how could she?

'I've done my first part of anaesthetic training,' she said, diffidently now. 'Finding veins is what I'm good at.'

'You're an anaesthetist?'

'Nearly. You didn't know that, did you, Dr Denver?' To his further astonishment, she sounded smug. 'Emergency physician with anaesthetist skills. You have two medics for the price of one. So…can I help?'

And he looked again at Horace's arm and he thought of the consequences of not trusting. She was an anaesthetist. They were both in impossible positions but she had the training.

'Yes, please.'

Her hands hurt. Lowering herself using only the thin cord had been rough.

Her backside also hurt. Three thin nylon cords weren't anyone's idea of good seat padding. She was using her feet to swing herself as close to the truck as she dared, trying to balance next to the window.

There was nothing to tie herself to.

And then Hugo reached over and caught the halter-tie of her dress, so her shoulder was caught at the rear of the window.

'No weight,' he told her. 'I'll just hold you steady.'

'What a good thing I didn't wear a strapless number,' she said approvingly, trying to ignore the feel of his hand against her bare skin. Truly, this was the most extraordinary position...

It was the most extraordinary feeling. His hold made her feel...safe?

Was she out of her mind? *Safe?* But he held fast and it settled her.

Hugo had swabbed but she swabbed again, holding Horace's arm steady as she worked. She had his arm out of the window, resting on the window ledge. The light here was good.

She pressed lightly and pressed again...

The cannula was suddenly in her hand. Hugo was holding her with one hand, acting as theatre assistant with the other.

Once again that word played into her mind. *Safe...* But she had eyes only for the faint contour that said she might have a viable vein...

She took the cannula and took a moment to steady herself. Hugo's hold on her tightened.

She inserted the point—and the needle slipped seamlessly into the vein.

'Yay, us,' she breathed, but Hugo was already handing her some sticking plaster to tape the cannula. She was checking the track, but it was looking good. A minute later she had the bag attached and fluid was flowing. She just might have done the thing.

Hugo let her go. She swung out a little, clear of the truck. It was the sensible thing to do, but still...

She hadn't wanted to be...let go.

'Heart rate?' Her voice wasn't quite steady. She took a deep breath and tried again. 'How is it?'

'Holding.' Hugo had his stethoscope out. 'I think we might have made it.' He glanced into the bag. 'And we have adrenaline—and a defibrillator. How did you carry all this?'

'I tied it under my seat.'

'Where did you learn your knots?'

'I was a star Girl Guide.' She was, too, she thought, deciding maybe she needed to focus on anything but the way his hold had made her feel.

A star Girl Guide... She'd been a star at so many things— at anything, really, that would get her away from her parents' overriding concern. Riding lessons, piano lessons, judo, elocution, Girl Guides, holiday camps... She'd been taken to each of them by a continuous stream of nannies. Nannies who were chosen because they spoke French, had famous relatives or in some other way could be boasted about by her parents...

'The current girl's a Churchill. She's au-pairing for six months, and she knows all the right people...'

Yeah. Nannies, nannies and nannies. Knowing the right people or speaking five languages was never a sign of job permanence. Polly had mostly been glad to be delivered to piano or elocution or whatever. She'd done okay, too. She'd had to.

Her parents loved her, but oh, they loved to boast.

'ER Physician, anaesthetist and Girl Guide to boot.' Hugo sounded stunned. 'I don't suppose you brought a stretcher as well? Plus a qualification in mountain rescue.'

'A full examination table, complete with lights, sinks, sterilisers? Plus rope ladders and mountain goats? Damn, I knew I'd forgotten something.'

He chuckled but she didn't have time for further banter. She was swinging in a way that was making her a little dizzy. She had to catch the sapling.

Her feet were hitting the cliff. *Ouch.* Where was nice soft grass when you needed it?

Where was Hugo's hold when she needed it?

He was busy. It made sense that he take over Horace's care now, but...

She missed that hold.

'It's flowing well.' There was no mistaking the satisfaction in Hugo's voice and Polly, too, breathed again. If Horace's heart hadn't given way yet, there was every chance the fluids would make a difference.

In the truck, Hugo had the IV line set up and secure. He'd hung the saline bags from an umbrella he'd wedged behind the back seat. He'd injected morphine.

He'd like oxygen but Polly's culling of his bag had excluded it. *Fair enough*, he thought. *Oxygen or a defibrillator?* With massive blood loss, the defibrillator was likely to be the most important, and the oxygen cylinder was dead weight.

Even so… How had she managed to get all this down here? What she'd achieved was amazing, and finding a vein in these circumstances was nothing short of miraculous.

She was his locum, temporary relief.

How would it be if there was a doctor like Polly working beside him in the Valley all year round?

Right. As if that was going to happen. His new locum was swinging on her seat, as if flying free, and he thought that was exactly what she was. *Free.*

Not trapped, like he was.

And suddenly he wasn't thinking trapped in a truck down a cliff. He was thinking trapped in Wombat Valley, giving up his career, giving up…his life.

Once upon a time, if he'd met someone like Dr Polly Hargreaves he could have asked her out, had fun, tried friendship and maybe it could have led to…

No! It was no use even letting himself think down that road.

He was trapped in Wombat Valley. The skilful, intriguing Polly Hargreaves was rescuing him from one trap.

No one could rescue him from the bigger one.

Fifteen minutes later, help arrived. *About time too*, Polly thought. Mountains were for mountain goats. When the first yellow-jacketed figure appeared at the cliff top it was all she could do not to weep with relief.

She didn't. She was a doctor and doctors didn't weep.

Or not when yellow coats and big boots and serious equipment were on their way to save them.

'We have company,' she announced to Hugo, who couldn't see the cliff top from where he was stuck.

'More polka dots?'

She grinned and looked up at the man staring down at her. 'Hi,' she yelled. 'Dr Denver wants to know what you're wearing.'

The guy was on his stomach, looking down. 'A business suit,' he managed. 'With matching tie. How'd you get down there?'

'They fell,' she said. 'I came down all by myself. You wouldn't, by any chance, have a cushion?'

He chuckled and then got serious. The situation was assessed with reassuring efficiency. There was more than one yellow jacket up there, it seemed, but only one was venturing near the edge.

'We'll get you up, miss,' the guy called.

'Stabilise the truck first.'

'Will do.'

The Australian State Emergency Service was a truly awesome organisation, Polly decided. Manned mostly by volunteers, their skill set was amazing. The police sergeant had arrived, too, as well as two farmers with a tractor apiece. Someone had done some fast organising.

Two yellow-jacketed officers abseiled down, with much more efficiency and speed than Polly could have managed. They had the truck roped in minutes, anchoring it to the tractors above.

They disappeared again.

'You think they've knocked off for a cuppa?' Polly asked Hugo and he smiled, but absently. His smile was strained.

He had a kid, Polly thought. What was he about, putting himself in harm's way?

Did his wife know where he was? If she did, she'd be having kittens.

Just lucky no one gave a toss about her.

Ooh, there was a bitter thought, and it wasn't true. Her parents would be gutted. But then... If she died they could organise a truly grand funeral, she decided. If there was one thing her mother was good at, it was event management. There'd be a cathedral, massed choirs, requests to wear *'Polly's favourite colour'* which would be pink because her mother always told her pink was her favourite colour even though it wasn't. And she'd arrange a release of white doves and pink and white balloons and the balloons would contain a packet of seeds—zinnias, she thought because *'they're Polly's favourite flower'* and...

And there was the roar of tractors from above, the sound of sharp commands, and then a slow taking up of the slack of the attached ropes.

The truck moved, just a little—and settled again—and the man appeared over the edge and shouted, 'You okay down there?'

'Excellent,' Hugo called, but Polly didn't say anything at all.

'Truck's now secure,' the guy called. 'The paramedics want to know if Horace is okay to move. We can abseil down and bring Horace up on a cradle stretcher. How does that fit with you, Doc?'

'Is it safe for you guys?'

'Go teach your grandmother to suck eggs,' the guy retorted. 'But med report, Doc—the paramedics want to know.'

'He's safe to move as long as we can keep pressure off his chest,' Hugo called. 'I want a neck brace. There's no sign of spinal injury but let's not take any chances. Then Polly.'

'Then you, Doc.'

'Polly second,' Hugo said in a voice that brooked no argument.

And, for once, Polly wasn't arguing.

* * *

It must have been under the truck.

She'd been balancing in the harness, using her feet to stop herself from swinging.

The truck had done its jerk upward and she'd jerked backwards herself, maybe as an automatic reaction to tension. She'd pushed her feet hard against the cliff to steady herself.

The snake must have been caught under the truck in the initial fall. With the pressure off, it lurched forward to get away.

Polly's foot landed right on its spine.

It landed one fierce bite to her ankle—and then slithered away down the cliff.

She didn't move. She didn't cry out.

Two guys in bright yellow overalls were abseiling down towards the driver's side of the truck, holding an end of a cradle stretcher apiece. They looked competent, sure of themselves…fast?

Horace was still the priority. He was elderly, he'd suffered massive blood loss and he needed to be where he could be worked on if he went into cardiac arrest.

She was suffering a snake bite.

Tiger snake? She wasn't sure. She'd only ever seen one in the zoo and she hadn't looked all that closely then.

It had had stripes.

Tiger snakes were deadly.

But not immediately. Wombat Valley was a bush hospital and one thing bush hospitals were bound to have was antivenin, she told herself. She thought back to her training. No one ever died in screaming agony two minutes after they were bitten by a snake. They died hours later. If they didn't get antivenin.

Therefore, she just needed to stay still and the nice guys in the yellow suits would come and get her and they'd all live happily ever after.

'Polly?' It was Hugo, his voice suddenly sharp.

'I…what?' She let go her toehold—she was only using one foot now—and her rope swung.

She felt…a bit sick.

That must be her imagination. She shouldn't feel sick so fast.

'Polly, what's happening?'

The guys—no, on closer inspection, it was a guy and a woman—had reached Horace. Had Hugo fitted the neck brace to Horace, or had the abseilers? She hadn't noticed. They were steadying the stretcher against the cliff, then sliding it into the cab of the truck, but leaving its weight to be taken by the anchor point on the road. In another world she'd be fascinated.

Things were a bit…fuzzy.

'Polly?'

'Mmm?' She was having trouble getting her tongue to work. Her mouth felt thick and dry.

'What the hell…? I can't get out. Someone up there…priority's changed. We need a harness on Dr Hargreaves—fast.'

Did he think she was going to faint? She thought about that and decided he might be right.

So do something.

She had a seat—sort of. She looped her arms around the side cords and linked her hands, then put her head down as far as she could.

She could use some glucose.

'Get someone down here.' It was a roar. 'Fast. Move!'

'I'm not going to faint,' she managed but it sounded feeble, even to her.

'Damn right, you're not going to faint,' Hugo snapped. 'You faint and you're out of my employ. Pull yourself together, Dr Hargreaves. Put that head further down, take deep breaths and count between breathing. You know what to do. Do it.'

'I need…juice…' she managed but her voice trailed off. This was ridiculous. She couldn't…

She mustn't.

Breathe, two, three. Out, two, three. Breathe...

'Hold on, sweetheart—they're coming.'

What had he called her? *Sweetheart?* No one called Polly Hargreaves sweetheart unless they wanted her to do something. Or not do something. Not to cut her hair. Not to do medicine. To play socialite daughter for their friends.

To come home for Christmas...

She wasn't going home for Christmas. She was staying in Wombat Valley. The thought was enough to steady her.

If she fainted then she'd fall and they'd send her back to Sydney in a body bag and her mother would have her fabulous funeral...

Not. Not, not, not.

'I've been bitten by a snake,' she muttered, with as much strength and dignity as she could muster. *Which wasn't actually very much at all.* She still had her head between her knees and she daren't move. 'It was brown with stripes and it bit my ankle. And I know it's a hell of a time to tell you, but I need to say...I'm also a Type One diabetic. So I'm not sure whether this is a hypo or snake bite but, if I fall, don't let my mother bury me in pink. Promise.'

'I promise,' Hugo said and then a yellow-suited figure was beside her, and her only objection was that he was blocking her view of Hugo.

It sort of seemed important that she see Hugo.

'She has a snake bite on her ankle,' Hugo was saying urgently. 'And she needs glucose. Probable hypo. Get the cradle back down here as fast as you can, and bring glucagon. While we wait, I have a pressure bandage here in the cabin. If you can swing her closer we'll get her leg immobilised.'

'You're supposed to be on holiday,' Polly managed while Yellow Suit figured out how to manoeuvre her closer to Hugo.

'Like that's going to happen now,' Hugo said grimly. 'Let's get the hired help safe and worry about holidays later.'

CHAPTER FOUR

FROM THERE THINGS moved fast. The team on the road was reassuringly professional. Polly was strapped into the cradle, her leg firmly wrapped, then she was lifted up the cliff with an abseiler at either end of the cradle.

She was hardly bumped, but she felt shaky and sick. If she was in an emergency situation she'd be no help at all.

'I'm so sorry,' she managed, for Hugo had climbed up after her and he was leaning over the stretcher, his lean, strong face creased in concern. 'What a wuss. I didn't mean...'

'To be confronted by two guys about to fall down a cliff. To need to climb down and secure the truck and save them. To bring them lifesaving equipment and get bitten by a snake doing it. I don't blame you for apologising, Dr Hargreaves. Wuss doesn't begin to describe it.'

'I should...'

'Shut up,' he said, quite kindly. 'Polly, the snake...you said it had stripes.'

'Brown with faint stripes.'

'Great for noticing.'

'It bit me,' she said with dignity. 'I always take notice of things that bite me.'

'Excellent. Okay, sweetheart, we have a plan...'

'I'm not your sweetheart!' She said it with vehemence and she saw his brows rise in surprise—and also humour.

'No. Inappropriate. Sexist. Apologies. Okay, Dr Hargreaves, we have a plan. We're taking you to the Wombat Valley Hospital—it's only a mile down the road. There we'll fill you up with antivenin. The snake you describe is either a tiger or a brown…'

'Tiger's worse.'

'We have antivenin for both. You're reacting well with glucose. I think the faintness was a combination—the adrenaline went out of the situation just as the snake hit and the shock was enough to send you over the edge.'

'I did not go over the edge!'

'I do need to get my language right,' he said and grinned. 'No, Dr Hargreaves, you did not go over the edge, for which I'm profoundly grateful. And now we'll get the antivenin in…'

'Which one?'

'I have a test kit at the hospital and I've already taken a swab.'

'And if it's a rare…I don't know…zebra python with no known antivenin…?'

'Then I'll eat my hat.' And then he took her hand and held, and he smiled down at her and his smile…

It sort of did funny things to her. She'd been feeling woozy before. Now she was feeling even woozier.

'We need to move,' he said, still holding her hand strongly. 'We'll take you to the hospital now, but once we have the antivenin on board we'll transfer you to Sydney. We've already called in the medical transfer chopper. Horace has cracked ribs. Marg's demanding specialists. I'm more than happy that he be transferred, and I'm imagining that you'll be' better in Sydney as well. You have cuts and bruises all over you, plus a load of snake venom. You can recover in Sydney and then spend Christmas with your family.'

Silence.

He was still holding her hand. She should let it go, she thought absently. She should push herself up to standing, put her hands on her hips and let him have it.

She was no more capable of doing such a thing than flying, but she gripped his hand so tightly her cuts screamed in protest. She'd bleed on him, she thought absently, but what was a little gore when what she had to say was so important?

'I am not going back to Sydney,' she hissed and she saw his brow snap down in surprise.

'Polly...'

'Don't Polly me. If you think I've come all this way...if you think I've crawled down cliffs and ruined a perfectly good dress and scratched my hands and hurt my bum and then been bitten by a vicious, lethal snake you don't even know the name of yet...if you think I'm going to go through all that and still get to spend Christmas in Sydney...'

'You don't want to?' he asked cautiously and she stared at him as if he had a kangaroo loose in his top paddock.

'In your dreams. I accepted a job in Wombat Valley and that's where I'm staying. You do have antivenin?'

'I...yes.'

'And competent staff to watch my vital signs for the next twenty-four hours?'

'Yes, but...'

'But nothing,' she snapped. 'You employed me, Dr Denver, and now you're stuck with me. Send Horace wherever you like, but I'm staying here.'

The transfer to the hospital was swift and efficient. Joe, his nurse administrator, was pre-warned and had the test kit and antivenin ready. Joe was more than capable of setting up an IV line. Wishing he was two doctors and not one, Hugo left Polly in Joe's care while he organised an X-ray of Horace's chest. He needed to make sure a rib wasn't about to pierce a lung.

The X-ray showed three cracked ribs, one that looked unstable. It hadn't punctured his lung, though, and Horace's breathing seemed secure. If he was kept immobile, he could be taken to Sydney.

'You're not sending Dr Hargreaves with him?' Mary, his

second-in-command nurse, demanded as he left Horace with the paramedics and headed for Polly.

He'd been torn... Polly, Horace, Polly, Horace...

Joe would have called him if there was a change. Still, his strides were lengthening.

'She won't go,' he told Mary. 'She wants to stay.'

'Oh, Hugo.' Mary was in her sixties, a grandma, and a bit weepy at the best of times. Now her kindly eyes filled with tears. 'You'll be looking after her instead of going to the beach. Of all the unfair things...'

'It's not unfair. It's just unfortunate. She can hardly take over my duties now. She'll need to be watched for twenty-four hours for reaction to the bite as well as reaction to the antivenin. The last thing we need is anaphylactic shock and it'll take days for the venom to clear her system completely. Meanwhile, have you seen her hands? Mary, she slid down a nylon cord to bring me equipment. She was scratched climbing to secure the truck. She was bitten because...'

'Because she didn't have sensible shoes on,' Mary said with asperity. The nurse was struggling to keep up but speed wasn't interfering with indignation. 'Did you see her shoes? Sergeant Myer picked them up on the roadside and brought them in. A more ridiculous pair of shoes for a country doctor to be wearing...'

'You think we should yell at her about her shoes?'

'I'm just saying...'

'She was driving here in her sports car. You don't need sensible clothes while driving.'

'Well, that's another thing,' Mary said darkly. 'Of all the silly cars for a country GP...'

'But she's not a country GP.' He turned and took a moment to focus on Mary's distress. Mary was genuinely upset on his behalf—heck, the whole of Wombat Valley would be upset on his behalf—but Polly wasn't to blame and suddenly it was important that the whole of Wombat Valley knew it.

He thought of Polly sitting on her makeshift swing, trying

to steady herself with her bare feet. He thought of her polka dot dress, the flounces, the determined smile… She must have been hurting more than he could imagine—those cords had really cut—but she'd still managed to give him cheek.

He thought of her sorting the medical equipment in his bag, expertly discarding what wasn't needed, determined to bring him what was. Courage didn't begin to describe what she'd done, he thought, so no, he wasn't about to lecture her for inappropriate footwear.

'Polly saved us,' he told Mary, gently but firmly. 'What happened was an accident and she did more than anyone could expect. She put her life on the line to save us and she even managed her own medical drama with skill. I owe her everything.'

'So you'll miss your Christmas at the beach.'

'There's no choice. We need to move on.'

Mary sniffed, sounding unconvinced, but Hugo swung open the door of the treatment room and Joe was chuckling and Polly was smiling up and he thought…

Who could possibly judge this woman and find her wanting? Who could criticise her?

This woman was amazing—and it seemed that she, also, was moving on.

'Doctor, we may have to rethink the hospital menu for Christmas if Dr Hargreaves is admitted,' Joe told him as he entered. 'She's telling me turkey, three veggies, commercial Christmas pudding and canned custard won't cut it. Not even if we add a bonbon on the side.'

He blinked.

Snake bite. Lacerations. Shock.

They were talking turkey?

Okay. He needed to focus on medical imperatives, even if his patient wasn't. Even if Polly didn't seem like his patient.

'The swab?' he asked and Joe nodded and held up the test kit.

'The brown snake showed up in seconds. The tiger segment showed positive about two minutes later but the kit says that's often the way—they're similar. It seems the brown snake venom's enough to eventually discolour the tiger snake pocket, so brown it is. And I reckon she's got a fair dose on board. Polly has a headache and nausea already. I'm betting she's been solidly bitten.'

Hugo checked the kit for himself and nodded. He'd seen the ankle—it'd be a miracle if the venom hadn't gone in. 'Brown's good,' he told Polly. 'You'll recover faster than from a tiger.'

'I'm feeling better already,' she told him and gave him another smile, albeit a wobbly one. 'But not my dress. It's ripped to pieces. That snake owes me...'

He had to smile. She even managed to sound indignant.

'But you're nauseous?'

'Don't you care about my dress?'

'I care about you more. Nausea?'

'A little. And,' she went on, as if she was making an enormous concession, 'I might be a little bit headachy.'

A little...

The venom would hardly be taking effect yet, he thought. She'd still be in the window period where victims ran for help, tried to pretend they hadn't been bitten, tried to search and identify the snake that had bitten them—and in the process spread the venom through their system and courted death.

Polly had been sensible, though. She'd stayed still. She'd told him straight away. She'd allowed the paramedics to bring her up on the rigid stretcher.

Okay, clambering down cliffs in bare feet in the Australian summer was hardly sensible but he couldn't argue with her reasons.

'Then let's keep it like that,' he told her. 'I want you to stay still while we get this antivenin on board.'

'I've been practically rigid since I got bit,' she said virtuously. 'Textbook patient. By the way, it's a textbook immobilisation bandage too. Excellent work, Dr Denver.'

He grinned at that, and she smiled back at him, and then he sort of paused.

That smile...

It was a magic smile. As sick and battered as she was, her smile twinkled. Her face was pallid and wan, but it was still alight with laughter.

This was a woman who would have played in the orchestra as the *Titanic* sank, he thought, and then he thought: *Nope*, she'd be too busy fashioning lifelines out of spare trombones.

But her smile was fading. Their gazes still held but all of a sudden she looked...doubtful?

Maybe unsure.

Maybe his smile was having the same effect on her as hers was on his?

That would be wishful thinking. Plus it would be unprofessional.

Move on.

Joe had already set up the drip. Hugo prepared the serum, double-checked everything with Joe, then carefully injected it. It'd start working almost immediately, he thought; hopefully, before Polly started feeling the full effects of the bite.

'How are you feeling everywhere else?' he asked, and she gave a wry smile that told him more than anything else that the humour was an act. Her freckles stood out from her pallid face, and her red hair seemed overbright.

'I'm...sore,' she admitted.

'I've started cleaning the worst of the grazes,' Joe told him. 'She could do with a full bed bath but you said immobile so immobile it is. There's a cut on her palm, though, that might need a stitch or two.'

He lifted her palm and turned it over. And winced.

Her hand was a mess. He could see the coil marks of the

rope. The marks ran along her palm, across her wrist and up her arm.

She'd come down that nylon cord…

He heard Mary's breath hiss in amazement. 'How…?'

'I told you,' he said, still staring at Polly's palm. 'She let herself down the cliff, carrying the bag with saline. Without it, Horace would probably be dead.'

'You did that for Horace?' Mary breathed, looking at the mess in horror, and Hugo thought he no longer had to defend her. Polly had suddenly transformed into a heroine.

'There's a lot to be said for elevators,' Polly said but her voice faltered a little as she looked at her palm and he re-alised shock was still a factor.

And there'd be bruises everywhere. He had to get that antivenin working, though, before they could clean her up properly. Joe had even left the remnants of her dress on. The polka dots made her look even more wan.

'Let's get you comfortable,' he said. 'How about a nice dose of morphine for the pain, some metoclopramide for the nausea and a wee shot of Valium on the side?'

'You want to knock me into the middle of next week?'

'I want you to sleep.'

She gazed up at him, those amazing eyes locked to his. He couldn't make out whether they were green or brown. They were…

Um…no. She was his patient. He didn't note the colour of his patient's eyes unless there was a medical issue. Blood-shot? Jaundiced? Fixed pupils? Polly's eyes showed none of those. He needed to ignore them.

How could he ignore them?

'You promise you won't transport me to Sydney while I'm sleeping?' she demanded, and he smiled and kept look-ing into those over-bright eyes.

'I promise.'

'That's in front of witnesses.'

'Joe, Mary, you heard me. The lady stays in Wombat Valley.'

'Very well, then,' Polly said, her voice wobbling again. Still, she looked straight up at him, as if reading reassurance in his gaze. 'Drugs, drugs and more drugs, and then Christmas in Wombat Valley. I can… I can handle that. But turkey with three veg has to go, Dr Denver.'

'You'll get a better Christmas dinner in Sydney.'

'No Sydney! Promise?'

'I already have,' he told her but suddenly she was no longer listening. The fight had gone out of her. She had the antivenin on board. Her future was sorted.

The flight-or-fight reflex relaxed. She sank back onto the pillows and sighed.

'Okay, Dr Denver, whatever you say,' she whispered. 'I'm in your hands.'

He had Horace sorted. He had Polly comfortable.

There was still the issue of Ruby.

How did you tell a seven-year-old she wasn't going to the beach for Christmas? She'd been counting down the days for months. He'd tried to figure it out all the way back to the house, but in the end he didn't need to.

Lois, his housekeeper, was before him. News got around fast in Wombat Valley and by the time he walked in the front door, Ruby was in tears and Lois was looking like a martyr who'd come to the end of her tether.

'I'm sorry, Dr Denver, but I can't stay,' she told him over the top of Ruby's head. 'I promised my son I'd spend Christmas in Melbourne with my grandchildren and that's where I'm going. I leave in half an hour, and I've told Ruby you're not going anywhere. You can see how upset she is, but is it my fault? You went and climbed into that truck. Was Horace worth it? He's a lazy wastrel and his wife's no better. Risking your life, losing your holiday, for such a loser…' She shook her head. 'I wash my hands of you, I really do.

Ruby, stop crying, sweetheart. I dare say your uncle will sort something out.'

And she picked up her handbag and headed out of the house before Hugo could possibly change her mind.

Hugo was left facing his niece.

Christmas. No beach. No housekeeper.

One fill-in doctor in his hospital instead of in his surgery.

He was trapped, but what was new? What was new was that Ruby felt as if she was trapped with him.

His niece looked as if she'd been trying not to cry, but fat tears were sliding down her face regardless. She stood silent, in her garden-stained shorts and T-shirt, her wispy blonde curls escaping every which way from their pigtails, and her wan little face blank with misery. She didn't complain, though, he thought bleakly. She never had.

He knelt down and hugged her. She held her stiff little body in his arms and he felt the effort she was making not to sob.

'We'll fix it somehow,' he murmured. 'Somehow...'

How?

Today was Monday. Christmas was Saturday.

He thought of the gifts he'd already packed, ready to be produced by Santa at their apartment by the beach. Bucket and spade. Water wings. A blow-up seahorse.

Lois had even made her a bikini.

He thought of his housekeeper marching off towards her Christmas and he thought he couldn't blame her. Lois was fond of Ruby, but he'd pushed her to the limit.

And there was another complication. It was school holidays and Ruby would need daytime care if he had to keep working. He'd need to call in favours, and he hated asking for favours.

Maybe he and Ruby should just walk away, he thought bleakly, as he'd thought many times this past year. But the complications flooded in, as they always did.

Wombat Valley was Ruby's home. It was all she knew. In

Sydney she had nothing and no one but him. His old job, the job he loved, thoracic surgery at Sydney Central, involved long hours and call backs. Here, his house was right next to the hospital. He could pop in and out at will, and he had an entire valley of people more than willing to help. They helped not just because it meant the Valley had a doctor but because so many of them genuinely cared for Ruby.

How could *he* stop caring, when the Valley had shown they cared so much? How could he turn his back on the Valley's needs and on Ruby's needs?

How could he ever return to the work he loved, to his friends, his social life, to his glorious bachelor freedom?

He couldn't. He couldn't even leave for two weeks. He had patients in hospital.

He had Dr Pollyanna Hargreaves in Ward One.

Polly...

Why was Polly so important? What was he doing, hugging Ruby and drying her eyes but thinking of Polly? But the image of Polly, hanging on her appalling handmade swing while every part of her hurt, wouldn't go away.

'Ruby, I need to tell you about one brave lady,' he told her and Ruby sniffed and swiped away her tears with the back of her hand and tilted her chin, ready to listen. In her own way, she was as brave as Polly, he thought.

But not as cute. No matter how much the Valley mums helped, Ruby always looked a waif. She was skinny and leggy, and nothing seemed to help her put on weight. She was tall for her seven years; her skimpy pigtails made her look taller and her eyes always seemed too big for her face. Her knees were constantly grubby—she'd have been mucking about in the garden, which was her favourite place. She had mud on her tear-stained face.

He loved her with all his heart.

'Is the lady why we can't go to the beach?' she quavered and he took her hand and led her out to the veranda. And there was another reminder of what they'd be missing. Hamster wasn't there.

Hamster was Ruby's Labrador, a great boofy friend. They hadn't been able to find a beach house where dogs were permitted so he'd taken Hamster back to the farmer who'd bred him, to be taken care of for two weeks.

Ruby had sobbed.

There was one bright thought—they could get Hamster back for Christmas.

Meanwhile, he had to say it like it was.

'Did Lois tell you about the truck accident?' he asked and Ruby nodded. She was a quiet kid but she listened. He'd learned early it was impossible to keep much from her.

'Well, the truck fell off the cliff, and the lady doctor— Dr Hargreaves—the doctor who was coming to work here while we were away—hurt herself by climbing down the cliff to save everyone.'

Ruby's pixie face creased as she sorted it out in her head. 'Everyone?'

'Yes.'

'Why didn't you save everyone?'

'I tried but I got stuck. She saved me, too. And then she got bitten by a snake.'

Ruby's eyes widened. 'What sort of a snake?'

'A brown.'

'That's better than a tiger. Didn't she know to make a noise? If you make lots of noise they slither away before you reach them.'

'The snake got stuck under the truck. I guess it got scared too, and it bit her.'

'Is she very sick?'

'She'll be sick for a couple of days.'

'So then can we go to the beach?'

He thought about it. *Don't make promises*, he told himself, but if Polly didn't react too badly to the antivenin it might be possible. If those cuts didn't stop her working.

She still wanted to stay in the Valley.

'I'm not sure,' he said weakly.

'Will she have to stay in hospital all over Christmas?'

That was a thought. And a problem?

Normally, snake bite victims stayed in hospital overnight for observation. She was a Type One diabetic. She might need to stay longer, but she was already having reservations about hospital food. How long could he keep her there?

He and Ruby had cleared out their best spare room. They'd made it look pretty. Ruby had even put fresh flowers in a vase on the chest of drawers. 'Girls like that.'

But he couldn't leave the moment she was released from hospital, he conceded. He and Polly would have to stay for a day or two.

He was counting in his head. Monday today. Bring Polly back here on Tuesday or Wednesday.

Leave on Thursday or Friday? Christmas Saturday.

It was cutting things fine.

Food... There was another problem. Sick and shocked as she was, Polly Hargreaves had already turned her nose up at bought pudding.

He had no food here. He'd assumed his locum could eat in the hospital kitchen.

He'd promised Ruby fish and chips on the beach for Christmas, and Ruby had glowed at the thought. Now... He might well have a recovering Polly for Christmas.

He didn't even have a Christmas tree.

And, as if on cue, there was the sound of a car horn from the road—a silly, tooting car horn that was nothing like the sensible farm vehicle horns used for clearing cattle off the road or warning of kangaroos. He looked up and a little yellow sports car was being driven through the gate, a police car following behind.

This was Polly's car. He'd seen it at the crash site but he'd been too distracted to do more than glance at it.

But here it was, being driven by one of the local farmers. Bill McCray was behind the wheel, twenty-five years old and grinning like the Cheshire cat.

'Hey, Doc, where do you want us to put the car?'

'What's the car?' Ruby breathed.

'I... It's Polly's car,' he managed.

'Polly...'

'Dr Hargreaves...'

'Is that her name? Polly, like *Polly put the kettle on*?'

'I...yes.'

'It's yellow.' Ruby was pie-eyed. 'And it hasn't got a top. And it's got a Christmas tree in the back. And suitcases and suitcases.'

There were indeed suitcases and suitcases. And a Christmas tree. Silver. Large.

Bill pulled up under the veranda. Both he and the policeman emerged from their respective vehicles, Bill looking decidedly sorry the ride had come to an end.

'She's a beauty,' he declared. 'I'd love to see how the cows reacted if I tried to drive that round the farm. And the guys say the lady doc's just as pretty. I reckon I can feel a headache coming on. Or six. When did you say you were leaving, Doc?'

'We're not leaving,' Ruby whispered but she no longer sounded desolate. She was staring in stupefaction at the tree. It was all silver sparkles and it stretched over the top of the luggage, from the front passenger seat to well behind the exhaust pipe.

Polly had tied a huge red tinsel bow at the rear—to warn traffic of the long load? It looked...amazing.

'We're staying here to look after the lady doctor,' Ruby said, still staring. 'I think she might be nice. Is she nice, Uncle Hugo?'

'Very nice,' he said weakly and headed down to unpack a Christmas tree.

CHAPTER FIVE

NIGHT ROUND. HE SHOULD be eating fish and chips on the beach right now, Hugo thought as he headed through the darkened wards to Ward One. He'd thought he had this Christmas beautifully organised.

Most of his long-termers had gone home for Christmas. He had three elderly patients in the nursing home section, all with local family and heaps of visitors. None needed his constant attendance.

Sarah Ferguson was still in Room Two. Sarah had rolled a tractor on herself a month ago. She'd spent three weeks in Sydney Central and had been transferred here for the last couple of weeks to be closer to her family. Her family had already organised to have Christmas in her room. She hardly needed him either.

But Polly needed him. He'd been back and forth during the afternoon, checking her. Anaphylactic shock was still a possibility. He still had her on fifteen minute obs. She was looking okay but with snake bites you took no chances.

Barb, the night nurse, greeted him happily and put down her knitting to accompany him.

'I'm fine,' he told her. 'I can do my round by myself.'

The scarf Barb was knitting, a weird mix of eclectic colours, was barely six feet long. Barb had told him it needed to be ten.

'Why my grandson had to tell me he wanted a Dr Who scarf a week before Christmas…' she'd muttered last night and he'd thought he'd made things easy for her by keeping the hospital almost empty.

But Barb did take her job seriously. She was knitting in front of the monitors attached to Ward One, which acted as the Intensive Care room. Any blip in Polly's heart rate and she'd be in there in seconds, and one glance at the chart in front of her told him Polly had been checked thoroughly and regularly.

'No change?'

'She's not sleeping. She's pretty sore. If you could maybe write her up for some stronger pain relief for the night...' She hesitated. 'And, Doc... She's not admitting it but I'm sure she's still pretty shaken. She's putting on a brave front but my daughter's her age. All bravado but jelly inside.'

He nodded and left her to her knitting.

Polly's ward was in near darkness, lit only by the floor light. He knocked lightly and went in.

Polly was a huddled mass under the bedclothes. She'd drawn her knees up to her middle, almost in a foetal position.

She's still pretty shaken...

Barb was right, he thought. This was the age-old position for those alone and scared.

He had a sudden urge to head to the bed, scoop her up and hold her. She'd had one hell of a day. What she needed was comfort.

Someone to hold...

Um...that wouldn't be him. There were professional boundaries, after all.

Instead, he tugged the visitor's chair across to the bed, sat down and reached for her hand.

Um... Her wrist. Not her hand. He was taking her pulse. That was professional.

'Hey,' he said, very softly. 'How's it going?'

'Great,' she managed and he smiled. Her '*great*' had been weak but it was sarcastic.

Still she had spirit.

'The venom will have kicked in but the antivenin will be doing its job,' he told her. 'Your obs are good.'

'Like I said—great.' She eased herself from the foetal position, casually, as if she didn't want him to notice how she'd been lying. 'Sorry. That sounds ungrateful. I am grateful. Mary and Joe gave me a good wash. I'm antivenined. I'm stitched, I'm disinfected and I'm in a safe place. But I've ruined your holiday. I'm so sorry.'

All this and she was concerned about his missed vacation?

'Right,' he said, almost as sarcastic as she'd been. 'You saved my life and you're sorry.'

'I didn't save your life.'

'You know what happened when they tugged the truck up the cliff? It swung and hit one of the saplings that had been holding it from falling further. The sapling lifted right out of the ground. It'd been holding by a thread.'

She shuddered and his hold on her hand tightened. Forget taking her pulse, he decided. She needed comfort and he was giving it any way he could.

'Polly, is there anyone we can ring? The nurses tell me you haven't contacted anyone. Your parents? A boyfriend? Any friend?'

'You let my family know what's happened and you'll have helicopters landing on the roof in ten minutes. And the press. You'll have my dad threatening to sue you, the hospital and the National Parks for letting the Gap exist in the first place. You don't know my family. Please, I'm fine as I am.'

She wasn't fine, though. She still had the shakes.

The press? Who was she?

She was alone. That was all he needed to focus on right now. 'Polly, you need someone...'

'I don't need anyone.' She hesitated. 'Though I am a bit shaky,' she admitted. 'I could use another dose of that nice woozy Valium. You think another dose would turn me into an addict?'

'I think we can risk it. And how about more pain relief, too? I have a background morphine dose running in the IV line but we can top it up. Pain level, one to ten?'

'Six,' she said and he winced.

'Ouch. Why didn't you tell Barb? She would have got me here sooner.'

'I'm not a whinger.'

'How did I already know that?' He shook his head, re-checked her obs, rang for Barb and organised the drugs. Barb did what was needed and then bustled back to her scarf. That meant Hugo could leave too.

But Polly was alone and she was still shaking.

He could ask Barb to bring her knitting in here.

Then who would look after the monitors for the other rooms?

It was okay him being here, he decided. His house was right next door to the hospital and they had an intercom set up in the nurses' station, next to the monitors. Ruby had been fast asleep for a couple of hours but, any whimper she made, Barb would know and send him home fast.

So he could sit here for a while.

Just until Polly was asleep, he told himself. He sat and almost unconsciously she reached out and took his hand again. As if it was her right. As if it was something she really needed, almost as important as breathing.

'I was scared,' she admitted.

'Which part scared you the most?' he asked. 'Sliding down the cliff? Hanging on that nylon cord swing? When Joe Blake did his thing…?'

'Joe Blake?'

'You really are city,' he teased. 'Joe Blake—Snake.'

'It was a bad moment,' she confessed. 'But the worst was when I saw the truck. When I realised there were people in it.'

'I guess it'd be like watching stretchers being wheeled into Emergency after a car crash,' he said. 'Before you know what you're facing.'

'Yeah.'

'But you broke it into manageable bits. You have excellent triage skills, Dr Hargreaves.'

'Maybe.'

She fell silent for a minute and then the hold on his hand grew tighter. But what she said was at odds with her obvious need. 'You shouldn't be here,' she told him. 'You should be home with your niece. Barb tells me she's your niece and not your daughter and her name's Ruby. Is she home alone?'

'Home's next door. Her bedroom's a hundred yards from the nurses' station. Her nightlight's on and whoever's monitoring the nurses' station can watch the glow and can listen on the intercom. If Ruby wakes up, all she has to do is hit the button and she can talk to the nurses or to me.'

'Good system,' she said sleepily and he thought the drugs were taking effect—or maybe it was simply the promise of the drugs.

Or maybe it was because she was holding his hand? It seemed an almost unconscious action, but she wasn't letting go.

'Tell me about Ruby,' she whispered and he sat and thought about his niece and felt the pressure of Polly's hand in his and the sensation was…

Was what?

Something he didn't let himself feel. Something he'd pushed away?

'And tell me about you too,' she murmured and he thought he didn't need to tell her anything. Doctors didn't tell personal stuff to patients.

But in the silence of the little ward, in the peacefulness of the night, he found himself thinking about a night almost a year ago. The phone call from the police. The night he'd realised life as he knew it had just slammed to an end.

He'd been born and raised in this place—Wombat Valley, where nothing ever happened. Wombat Valley, where you could sit on the veranda at night and hear nothing but the frogs and the hoot of the night owls.

Wombat Valley, where everyone depended on everyone else.

Grace, his sister, had hated it. She'd run away at sixteen and she'd kept on running. 'I feel trapped,' she'd shouted, over and over. Hugo had been twelve when she'd run and he hadn't understood.

But twelve months ago, the night his sister died, it was Hugo who'd been trapped. That night he'd felt like running as well.

He didn't. How could he? He'd returned to the Valley and it seemed as if he'd be here for ever.

'Tell me about Ruby?' Polly whispered again, and her question wasn't impatient. It was as if the night had thoughts of its own and she was content to wait.

'Ruby's my niece.'

'Yeah. Something I don't know?'

'She's adorable.'

'And you wouldn't be biased?'

He smiled. She sounded half asleep, but she was still clutching his hand and he wondered if the questions were a ruse to have him stay.

'She's seven years old,' he said. 'She's skinny, tough, fragile, smart. She spends her time in the garden, mucking round in the dirt, trying to make things grow, playing with a menagerie of snails, tadpoles, frogs, ladybirds.'

'Her parents?'

'We don't know who her father is,' Hugo told her. He was almost talking to himself but it didn't seem to matter. 'My sister suffered from depression, augmented by drug use. She was always…erratic. She ran away at sixteen and we hardly saw her. She contacted me when Ruby was born—until then we hadn't even known she was pregnant. She was in Darwin and she was in a mess. I flew up and my parents followed.

Mum and Dad brought them both back to Wombat Valley. Grace came and went, but Ruby stayed.'

'Why…why the Valley?'

'My father was the Valley doctor—our current house is where Grace and I were raised. Dad died when Ruby was three, but Mum stayed on. Mum cared for Ruby and she loved her. Then, late last year, Grace decided she wanted to leave for good and she wanted Ruby back. She was with… someone who scared my mother. Apparently there was an enormous row, which culminated in Mum having a stroke. The day after Mum's funeral, Grace drove her car off the Gap. Maybe it was an accident. Probably it wasn't.'

'Oh, no…'

'So that's that,' he said flatly. 'End of story. The Valley loves Ruby, Ruby loves the Valley and I'm home for good. I'm not doing a great job with Ruby, but I'm trying. She loved Mum. Grace confused her and at the end she frightened her. Now she's too quiet. She's a tomboy. I worry…'

'There's nothing wrong with being a tomboy,' Polly whispered, sounding closer and closer to sleep. 'You don't force her to wear pink?'

He smiled at that. 'She'd have it filthy in minutes. What I should do is buy camouflage cloth and find a dungaree maker.'

'She sounds my type of kid.'

'You do pretty.'

Where had that come from? He shouldn't comment on patients' appearances. *You do pretty*? What sort of line was that?

'I like clothes that make me smile,' she whispered. 'I have an amazing pair of crimson boots. One day I might show you.'

'I'll look forward to that.' Maybe he shouldn't have said that either. Was it inappropriate?

Did he care?

'So Ruby knows she's safe with you?' she whispered.

'She's as safe as I can make her. We had an interim doctor after Dad died but he left the moment I appeared on the scene. This valley could use three doctors, but for now I'm it. I've been advertising for twelve months but no one's applied. Meanwhile, Ruby understands the intercom system and she can see the hospital from her bedroom. If I can't be there in ten seconds someone else will be. That's the deal the hospital board employs me under. Ruby comes first.'

'So if there's drama...'

'This community backs me up. I'm here if, and only if, Wombat Valley helps me raise Ruby.' He shrugged. 'It's my job.'

Only it wasn't, or not his job of choice. He'd walked away from his job as a thoracic surgeon. Not being able to use the skills he'd fought to attain still left him feeling gutted, and now he couldn't even get Christmas off.

'But I've so messed with your Christmas,' she said weakly, echoing his thoughts, and he hauled himself together.

'I've told you—you've done no such thing.'

'Would it be better for you if I was transferred?'

'I...no.'

'But I'm supposed to be staying in your house. You won't want me now.'

At least he had this answer ready. He'd had the evening to think about it. Polly's tree was now set up in the living room. He was preparing to make the most of it.

'If you stay, you might still be able to help me,' he said diffidently, as if he was asking a favour. And maybe he was; it was just that his ideas about this woman were all over the place and he couldn't quite get them together. 'You'll need a few days to get over your snake bite and bruises. You could snuggle into one of our spare rooms—it's a big house—and Ruby could look after you. She'd enjoy that.'

'Ruby would look after me?'

'She loves to be needed. She's already fascinated by your

snake bite—you'll have to show her the fang marks, by the way. She's also in love with your Christmas tree.'

'My tree...'

'The boys brought your car to my house. Ruby insisted we unpack it. I'm sorry but it's in the living room and Ruby's already started decorating it.'

'You don't have a tree of your own?'

'We were going away for Christmas.'

'You still should have had a tree,' she murmured, but her voice was getting so weak he could hardly hear. She was slurring her words and finally the hold on his hand was weakening. The drugs were taking over.

He should tuck her hand under the covers, he thought, and finally he did, but as he released her fingers he felt an indefinable sense of loss.

And, as he did, she smiled up at him, and weirdly she shifted her hand back out of the covers. She reached up and touched his face. Just lightly. It was a feather-touch, tracing the bones of his cheek.

'I'm glad I saved you,' she whispered and it was all he could do to hear.

'I'm glad you saved me too.' And for the life of him he couldn't stop a shake entering his voice.

'And you didn't have a Christmas tree...'

'N...no.'

'And now I'm going to stay with you until Christmas?'

What could he say? 'If you like.'

'Then it sounds like I need to be helpful,' she whispered, and it was as if she was summoning all the strength she had to say something. 'Sometimes I can be my mother's daughter. December the twentieth and you don't even have a tree. And you have a little girl who likes tadpoles and dungarees. And I just know you're a very nice man. What were you doing in that truck in the first place? The snake could just as easily have bitten you. You know what, Dr Denver? As well as saving your skin, I'm going to save your Christmas. How's that for a plan?'

But she got no further. Her hand fell away. Her lids closed, and she was asleep.

He walked home feeling...disorientated. Or more. Discombobulated? There was no other word big enough to describe it.

He could still feel the touch of Polly's fingers on his face where she'd touched him.

He might just as well have been kissed...

There was a crazy idea. He hadn't been kissed. She'd been doped to the eyeballs with painkillers and relaxants. She'd had an appalling shock and she was injured. People did and said weird things...

Still the trace of her fingers remained.

She was beautiful.

She was brave, funny, smart.

She was scared and she was alone.

But what had she said? He replayed her words in his head.

'You let my family know what's happened and you'll have helicopters landing on the roof ten minutes later. And the press...'

Who was she? He needed to do some research. He'd rung her medical referees when she'd applied to do the locum. He'd been given glowing reports on her medical skills but there'd been a certain reticence...

He'd avoided the reticence. He'd been so relieved to find a doctor with the skills to look after the Valley, he wouldn't have minded if she'd had two heads. If she had the medical qualifications, nothing else could matter.

Only of course it mattered and now he was stuck in the same house as a woman who was brave, funny and smart.

And beautiful.

And alone.

He didn't need this, he told himself. The last thing he

needed in his life was complications caused by a beautiful woman. A love life was something he'd left very firmly in Sydney. No complications until he had his little niece settled...

Right. Regardless, he reached the veranda, sat on the steps and typed her name into his phone's Internet app.

It took time for anything to show. His phone connection was slow. He should go inside and use his computer, but inside the door were Polly's suitcases, and in the living room was Polly's tree. For some reason he felt as if he needed to know what he was letting himself in for before he stepped over the threshold.

And here it was. Pollyanna Hargreaves.

She had a whole Wikipedia entry of her own.

Good grief!

Only child of Charles and Olivia Hargreaves. Expected to inherit the giant small goods manufacturing business built up by her family over generations. Currently practising medicine. Aged twenty-nine. One broken relationship, recent...

He snapped his phone shut. He didn't want to read any more.

What was she doing here? What was she running from?

The broken relationship?

What was she doing being a doctor?

Why didn't she want to go back to Sydney?

He should insist she go back. She could no longer do the job he was paying her for. She deserved compensation—of course she did—but his medical insurance would cover it. He could discharge her from hospital tomorrow or the next day, organise a driver and send her home.

She didn't want to spend Christmas in Sydney.

He sat on the step and stared into the night. The decision should be easy, he thought. She couldn't do the job she'd come for. He and Ruby were still living in the house. She couldn't stay here, so he could send her home.

Her Christmas tree was already up in the living room. This was a big house. They had room.

What was he afraid of?

Of the way she made him feel?

For heaven's sake... He was a mature thirty-six-year-old doctor. He'd had girlfriends in Sydney, one of them long-term. He and Louise had even talked marriage, but she'd been appalled at the idea of Wombat Valley and Ruby. He couldn't blame her.

If he wanted to move on...

On to Polly?

He shook his head in disbelief. This was crazy. He'd known her for less than a day. She was an heiress and she was his patient.

She was funny and smart and brave.

And beautiful.

And he was nuts. He rose and gave himself a fast mental shake. He'd been thrown about too today, he reminded himself. He had the bruises to prove it. There'd been a moment when he'd thought there was a fair chance he could have left Ruby without any family and that moment was still with him.

He must have been hit on the head, he decided, or be suffering from delayed shock. Something was messing with his head.

Polly was a patient tonight, and tomorrow or the next day she'd be staying here as a guest and then hopefully she'd be a colleague. The jury was still out on whether she'd be well enough to take over so he and Ruby could spend a few days at the beach, but if he sent her back to Sydney he'd never know.

He could still feel the touch of her hand...

'So get over it,' he told himself. He needed Hamster. Ruby's big Labrador, given to her as a puppy in desperation on that last appalling Christmas, had turned into his confidante, someone to talk to in the small hours when life got bleak.

He'd fetch Hamster back tomorrow.

And Polly. Polly and Hamster and Christmas.

If she was still here... If he couldn't leave... He'd have to find a turkey.

He didn't know how to cook a turkey.

Turkey. Bonbons. Christmas pudding. Ruby was old enough to know what Christmas dinner should be. She'd been happy with her beach fish and chips substitute, but now...

'Maybe Dr Hargreaves will know how to cook a turkey,' he said morosely but then he glanced again at the information on his phone.

Heiress to a fortune...

'Maybe she has the funds to fly one in ready cooked from Sydney,' he told the absent Hamster.

Maybe pigs could fly.

Polly woke, some time in the small hours.

She hurt.

What was it with snake bite? she wondered. Why did it make everything ache?

Maybe she should write this up for her favourite medical journal—disseminated pain after accidental infusion of snake venom.

That sounded impressive. Her father would show that to his golf cronies.

Her mother, though...she could just hear her. 'Who are you trying to impress? You'll never get a husband if you keep trying to be clever.'

She winced. Her hand hurt.

Okay, maybe this wasn't disseminated pain from infusion of snake venom. Maybe this was disseminated pain from abseiling down a cliff with nylon cord and bare feet.

Her mother might like that better. It didn't sound clever at all.

Why did she feel like crying?

She should ring the bell. She would in a moment, she told herself. The nice night nurse would arrive and top up her medication and send her back into a nice dozy sleep. But for now...

For now she wanted to wallow.

She was missing...missing...

The doctor with the strong, sure hands. Hugo Denver, who'd sat with her until she'd slept. Whose voice was nice and deep and caring. Who looked a million dollars—tall, dark, strong.

Who made her feel safe.

And there was a nonsense. She was always safe. If she let them, her parents would have her cocooned in protective luxury, buffered from the world, safe in their gorgeous lifestyle for ever.

Marrying Marcus.

She winced and shifted in bed and hurt some more, but still she didn't call Barb. She felt as if she had things to sort, and now was as good a time as any to sort them.

She was staying here—for Christmas, at least. Hugo Denver owed her that. But afterwards... What then?

Overseas...

Maybe some volunteer organisation. Doctors were needed everywhere and heaven knew she didn't need money.

Her parents would have kittens.

Her parents were currently having kittens because she wasn't in Sydney. If they knew she was in trouble...

They'd come and she didn't want them to come. She did not want family.

Whereas if Hugo Denver walked in the door...

What was she thinking? She was falling for her boss? Or her doctor? Each was equally unethical.

So why did she want him to come back? When she'd woken, why had her gaze gone directly to the place where he'd been sitting?

Why could she still feel his hand?

Weakness, she told herself and had to fight back a sudden urge to burst into tears. Weakness and loneliness.

She had no reason to be lonely. She had her parents' world ready to enfold her, a world she'd had to fight to escape from.

It'd be so easy to give in. Her parents loved her. One phone call and they'd be here. She'd be whisked back to the family mansion in Sydney. She'd be surrounded by private nurses and her mother would be popping in every twenty minutes with so much love she couldn't handle it.

Love...

Why was she thinking of Hugo Denver?

'Because you're a weak wuss and he has a smile to die for,' she told herself. 'And you've been battered and cut and bitten and you're not yourself. Tomorrow you'll be back to your chirpy self, defences up, self-reliant, needing no one.'

But if Hugo came back...

'Dr Denver to you,' she said out loud. 'A bit of professionalism, if you please, Dr Hargreaves.' She wiggled again and things hurt even more and she got sensible.

She rang the bell for a top-up of morphine. She didn't need Hugo Denver. Morphine would have to do instead.

CHAPTER SIX

HUGO ARRIVED IN her room at eleven in the morning, with Joe beside him. It was a professional visit: doctor doing his rounds with nurse in attendance. That was what Hugo looked—professional.

When she'd first seen him he'd been wearing casual clothes—dressed to go on holiday. Jeans and open-necked shirt. He'd been bloodied and filthy.

He'd come in last night but she couldn't remember much about last night. She'd been woozy and in pain. If she had to swear, she'd say he'd been wearing strength and a smile that said she was safe.

This morning he was in tailored pants and a crisp white shirt. The shirt was open-necked and short-sleeved. He looked professional but underneath the professional there was still the impression of strength.

Mary had helped her wash and Joe had brought one of her cases in. She was therefore wearing a cute kimono over silk pyjamas. She was ready to greet the world.

Sort of. This man had her unsettled.

The whole situation had her unsettled. She'd been employed to replace this man. What were the terms of her employment now?

'Hey,' he said, pausing at the door—giving her time to catch her breath? 'Joe tells me you're feeling better. True?'

She was. Or she had been. Now she was just feeling... disconcerted. Hormonal?

Interested.

Why? He wasn't her type, she thought. He looked...a bit

worn around the edges. He was tall, lean and tanned, all good, all interesting, but his black hair held a hint of silver and there were creases around his eyes. Life lines. Worry? Laughter? Who could tell?

He was smiling now, though, and the creases fitted, so maybe it was laughter.

He was caring for his niece single-handedly. He was also the face of medicine for the entire valley.

Her research told her the hospital had a huge feeder population. This was a popular area to retire and run a few head of cattle or grow a few vines. Retirees meant ageing. Ageing meant demand for doctor's services.

Hence the hint of silver?

Or had it been caused by tragedy? Responsibility?

Responsibility. *Family.*

He wasn't her type at all.

Meanwhile he seemed to be waiting for an answer. Joe had handed him her chart. He'd read it and was now looking at her expectantly. What had he asked? For some reason she had to fight to remember what the question had been.

Was she feeling better? She'd just answered herself. Now she had to answer him.

'I'm good,' she said, and then added a bit more truthfully, 'I guess I'm still a bit wobbly.'

'Pain?'

'Down to fell-over-in-the-playground levels.'

'You do a lot of falling over in the playground?'

'I ski,' she said and he winced.

'Ouch.'

'You don't?'

'There's not a lot of skiing in Wombat Valley.'

'But before?'

'I don't go back to before,' he said briskly. 'Moving on… Polly, what happens next is up to you. We have a guest room made up at home. Ruby's aching to play nurse, but if you're more settled here then we'll wait.'

Uh oh. She hadn't thought this through. She'd demanded she stay in Wombat Valley. She'd refused to be evacuated to Sydney, but now…

'I'm an imposition,' she said ruefully, and his grin flashed out again. Honestly, that grin was enough to make a girl's toes curl.

He wasn't her type. *He was not.*

'You're not an imposition,' he said gently. 'Without you I'd be down the bottom of the Gap, and Christmas would be well and truly over. As it is, my niece is currently making paper chains to hang on your truly amazing Christmas tree. I advertised for a locum. What seems to have arrived is a life-saver and a Santa. Ruby would love you to come home. We'll both understand if you put it off until tomorrow but the venom seems to have cleared. Joe tells me your temperature, pulse, all vital signs, are pretty much back to normal. You'll still ache but if you come home you get to spend the rest of the day in bed as well. We have a view over the valley to die for, and Ruby's waiting.'

His voice gentled as he said the last two words and she met his gaze and knew, suddenly, why his voice had changed. There was a look…

He loved his niece.

Unreservedly. Unconditionally.

Why did that make her eyes well up?

It was the drugs, she thought desperately, and swiped her face with the back of her hand, but Hugo reached over and snagged a couple of tissues and tugged her hand down and dried her face for her.

'You're too weak,' he said ruefully. 'This was a bad idea. Snuggle back to sleep for the day.'

But she didn't want to.

Doctors made the worst patients. That was true in more ways than one, she thought. Just like it'd kill a professional footballer to sit on the sidelines and watch, so it was for doctors. Plus she'd had a childhood of being an inpatient. Once her diabetes had been diagnosed, every time she sneezed her parents had insisted on admission. So now...all she wanted to do was grab her chart, fill it in herself, like the professional she was, and run.

Admittedly, she hadn't felt like that last night—with a load of snake venom on board, hospital had seemed a really safe option—but she did this morning.

'If you're happy to take me home, I'd be very grateful,' she murmured and he smiled as if he was truly pleased that he was getting a locum for Christmas, even if that locum had a bandaged hand and a bandaged foot and was useless for work for the foreseeable future.

'Excellent. Now?'

'I...yes.'

'Hugo, the wheelchairs are out of action for a couple of hours,' Joe volunteered, taking back the chart and hanging it on the bed. Looking from Hugo to Polly and back again with a certain amount of speculative interest. 'It's so quiet this week that Ted's taken them for a grease and oil change. They'll be back this afternoon but meanwhile Polly can't walk on that foot.'

'I can hop,' Polly volunteered and both men grinned.

'A pyjama-clad, kimono-wearing hoppity locum,' Joe said, chuckling. 'Wow, Hugo, you pick 'em.'

'I do, don't I?' Hugo agreed, chuckling as well and then smiling down at Polly. 'But no hoppiting. We don't need to wait. Polly, you're no longer a patient, or a locum. From now on, if you agree, you're our honoured guest, a colleague and a friend. And friends wearing battle scars won on our behalf get special treatment. Can I carry you?'

Could he...what?

Carry her. That was what the doctor had said.

She needed a wheelchair. She could wait.

That'd be surly.

Besides, she didn't want one. There was no way she

wanted to sit in a wheelchair and be pushed out feeling like a...patient.

She was a friend. Hugo had just said so.

But...but...

Those dark, smiling eyes had her mesmerised.

'I'll hurt your back,' she managed. 'I'm not looking after you in traction over Christmas.'

'I'm game if you are,' he said and his dark eyes gleamed. Daring her?

And all of a sudden she was in. Dare or not, he held her with his gaze, and suddenly, for this moment, Pollyanna Hargreaves wasn't a doctor. She wasn't a patient. She wasn't a daughter and actually...she wasn't a friend.

She was a woman, she thought, and she took a deep breath and smiled up into Hugo's gorgeous eyes.

He wanted to carry her?

'Yes, please.'

It was possibly not the wisest course to carry his new locum. His medical insurance company would have kittens if they could see him, he thought. He could drop her. He could fall. He could be sued for squillions. Joe, following bemusedly behind with Polly's suitcase, would act as witness to totally unethical behaviour.

But Polly was still shaky. He could hear it in her voice. Courageous as she'd been, yesterday had terrified her and the terror still lingered. She needed human contact. Warmth. Reassurance.

And Hugo... Well, if Hugo was honest, he wouldn't mind a bit of the same.

So he carried her and if the feel of her body cradled against him, warmth against warmth, if the sensation of her arms looped around his neck to make herself more secure, if both those things settled his own terrors from the day before then that was good. Wasn't it?

That was what this was all about, he told himself. Reassurance.

Except, as he strode out through the hospital entrance with his precious cargo, he felt...

As if he was carrying his bride over the threshold?

There was a crazy thought. Totally romantic. Nonsense.

'Where's your car?' she asked.

Polly's voice was still a bit shaky. He paused on the top of the ramp into Emergency and smiled down at her. The sun was on her face. Her flaming curls had been washed but they were tousled from a morning on her pillow. She had freckles. Cute freckles. Her face was a bit too pale and her green eyes a bit too large.

He'd really like to kiss her.

And that really was the way to get struck off any medical register he could care to name. Hire a locum, nearly kill her, carry her instead of using a wheelchair, then kiss her when she was stuck so tight in his arms she can't escape.

He needed a cold shower—fast.

'No car needed,' he said, and motioned towards a driveway along the side of the hospital.

At the end of the driveway there was a house, a big old weatherboard, looking slightly incongruous beside the newer brick hospital. It had an old-fashioned veranda with a kid's bike propped up by the door. A grapevine was growing under the roof, and a couple of Australia's gorgeous rosella parrots were searching through the leaves, looking for early grapes.

'This is home while you're in Wombat Valley,' he told her. 'But it won't be what you're used to. Speak now if you want to change your mind about staying. We can still organise transport out of here.'

'How do you know what I'm used to?' she asked and he grimaced and said nothing and she sighed. 'So I'm not incognito?'

'I don't think you could ever be incognito.'

She grimaced even more, and shifted in his arms. 'Hugo...'

'Mmm?'

'It's time to put me down. I can walk.'

'You're not walking.'

'Because I'm Pollyanna Hargreaves?'

'Because you have a snake-bitten ankle.'

'And you always carry snake-bite victims?'

'Oi!' It was Joe, standing patiently behind them, still holding the suitcase. 'In the time you've spent discussing it you could have taken her home, dumped her on the couch and got back here. I've work for you, Dr Denver.'

'What work?' Polly asked.

'Earache arriving in ten minutes,' Joe said darkly and glanced at his watch. 'No, make that in five.'

'Then dump me and run,' Polly said and he had no choice.

Like it or not, he had to dump her and run.

Ruby was waiting. Sort of.

He carried Polly over the threshold and Ruby was sitting on the couch in the front room, in her shorts and shirt, bare legs, tousled hair—she'd refused to let him braid it this morning—her face set in an expression he knew all too well. Misery.

He could hear Donna in the kitchen. Donna was a Wombat Valley mum. Donna's daughter, Talia, was Ruby's age, and Donna's family was just one of the emergency backstops Wombat Valley had put in place to make sure Hugo could stay here. He stood in the living room doorway, Polly in his arms, and looked helplessly down at his niece. When she looked like this he never knew what to say.

'We have a guest,' he said. 'Ruby, this is Dr Hargreaves.'

'Polly,' said Polly.

'Why are you carrying her?'

'She was bitten by a snake. I told you.'

'She's supposed to be working,' Ruby said in a small voice. 'And we're supposed to be at the beach.'

'Ruby…'

'It's the pits,' Polly interrupted. She was still cradled against him but she sounded ready to chat. 'Sorry, sorry, sorry,' she told the little girl. 'But we should blame the snake.'

'You should have been wearing shoes,' Ruby muttered, still in that little voice that spoke of the desolation of betrayal. Another broken promise.

'Yes,' Polly agreed. 'I should.'

'Why weren't you?'

'I didn't know I was planning to meet a snake, and it didn't warn me it was coming. They should wear bells, like cats.'

Ruby thought about that and found it wanting. 'Snakes don't have necks.'

'No.' Polly appeared thoughtful. 'We should do something about that. What if we made a rule that Australian snakes have to coil? If we had a law that every snake has to loop once so they have a circle where their neck should be, we could give them all bells. How are you at drawing? Maybe you could draw what we mean and we'll send a letter to Parliament this very day.'

Ruby stared at her as if she was a sandwich short of a picnic. 'A circle where their neck should be?' she said cautiously.

'If you have a skipping rope I'll show you. But we'd need to make it law, which means writing to Parliament. How about you do the drawing and I'll write the letter?'

Ruby stared at her in amazement. In stupefaction. The desolate expression on her face faded.

'"Dear Parliamentarians…",' Polly started. She was still ensconced in Hugo's arms, but she didn't appear to notice her unusual platform, or the fact that her secretary wasn't writing. 'It has come to our attention that snakes are slithering around the countryside bell-less. This situation is unsatisfactory, not only to people who wander about shoeless, but also to snakes who, we're sure, would be much happier with jewels. Imagine how much more Christmassy Australia would be if every snake wore a Christmas bell?'

And it was too much for Ruby.

She giggled.

It was the best sound in the world, Hugo thought. For twelve long months he'd longed to hear his niece giggle, and this woman had achieved it the moment she'd come through the door.

But the giggle was short-lived. Of course. He could see Ruby fight it, ordering her expression back to sad.

'You're still spoiling our Christmas,' she muttered.

'Not me personally,' Polly said blithely, refusing to sound offended. 'That was the snake. Put me down, Dr Denver. Ruby, can I share your couch? And thank you for putting up my Christmas tree. Do you like it?'

'Yes,' Ruby said reluctantly.

'Me too. Silver's my favourite.'

'I like real trees,' Hugo offered as he lowered Polly onto the couch beside his niece. 'Ones made out of pine needles.'

'Then why didn't you put one up?' Polly raised her brows in mock disapproval. She put her feet on the floor and he saw her wince. He pushed a padded ottoman forward; she put her foot on it and she smiled.

It was some smile.

'I know,' she said, carrying right on as if that smile meant nothing. 'You meant to be away for Christmas. That's no excuse, though. Trees are supposed to be decorated ages before Christmas. And you put all the presents for everyone from your teacher to the postman underneath, wrapped up mysteriously, and you get up every morning and poke and prod the presents and wonder if Santa's come early. It's half the fun.'

There was another fail. Add it to the list, Hugo thought morosely, but Polly had moved through accusatory and was now into fixing things.

'There's still time,' she said. 'Ruby, we can do some wrapping immediately. I'm stuck with this foot... Who's in the kitchen?'

'Mrs Connor,' Ruby muttered. 'She's cooking a Christmas cake 'cos she says if we're staying here we might need it.'

'Mrs Connor?' Polly queried.

'Talia's mum.'

'Talia's your friend?'

'Talia's at her grandma's place, making mince pies,' Ruby told her. 'She said I could come but I didn't want to. I don't have a grandma any more. My mum's dead too.'

But, despite the bleak words, Ruby was obviously fighting not to be drawn in by Polly's bounce. Hugo was fighting not to be drawn in, too. Polly was...magnetic. She was like a bright light and the moths were finding her irresistible.

What was he on about? He had work to do.

'I need to get on,' he said.

'I know. Earache.' Polly gave him a sympathetic smile. 'You could introduce me to Mrs Connor. Maybe she doesn't need to stay once her cake's cooked. Ruby and I can cope on our own. Do you have Christmas wrapping paper?'

He did get the occasional thing right. 'Yes.'

'Excellent. If you could find it for us...'

'We don't have anything to wrap,' Ruby said.

'Yes, we do. Have you ever heard of origami?'

'I...no,' she said cautiously.

'It's paper folding and I'm an expert.' Polly beamed. 'I can make birds and frogs that jump and little balls that practically float and tiny pretend lanterns. And I can make boxes to put them in. If you like I'll teach you and we can make presents for everyone in Wombat Valley. And then we'll wrap them in newspaper and make them really big and wrap them again in Christmas paper so no one will ever guess what's in them and then we'll stack them under the tree. Then we'll have presents for everyone who comes to the house or everyone in hospital or everyone in the main street of Wombat Valley if we make enough. Good idea or what, Ruby?'

'I...I'll watch,' Ruby said reluctantly and it was all Hugo

could do not to offer Polly a high five. *I'll watch...* Concession indeed.

'Then find us some wrapping paper and be off with you,' Polly told him. 'Ruby and I and Mrs Connor can manage without you.' And then she hesitated. 'Though...can you find me my jelly beans? They're in my holdall. And is there juice in the fridge?'

She was a diabetic. Of course. What was he thinking, not worrying about sources of instant sugar. Hell, why hadn't he left her in the hospital? And as for telling Donna to go home...

The weight of the last year settled back down hard. Two responsibilities...

But Polly was looking up at him and suddenly she was glaring. 'Do not look like that,' she snapped.

'Like what?'

'Like I'm needing help. I don't need help. I just need things to be in place.'

'If you have a hypo...'

'If I have my jelly beans and juice, I won't have a hypo.'

'How do you know? The snake bite...'

'Is your uncle a fusser?' Polly demanded, turning to Ruby. 'Does he fuss when you don't want him to?'

'He makes me have a bath every single day,' Ruby confessed. 'And I have to eat my vegetables.'

'I knew it. A fusser! Dr Denver, I will not be fussed over. A bath and vegetables for Ruby are the limit. I will not let you fuss further.'

'He'll get grumpy,' Ruby warned.

'Let him. I can cope with a grump.' And she tilted her chin and looked up at him, defiance oozing from every pore.

His lips twitched—and hers twitched in response.

'Jelly beans,' she repeated. 'Juice. Earache. Ruby—swans, lanterns, frogs?'

'Frogs,' Ruby said, watching her uncle's face.

He wasn't grumpy. He wasn't.

Maybe he had been a bit. Maybe this year had been enough to make anyone grumpy.

'Earth to Dr Denver,' Polly was saying. 'Are you reading? Jelly beans, juice, earache. Go.'

There was nothing else for it. A part of him really wanted to stay and watch...frogs?

Earache was waiting.

He had no choice. The demands on a lone family doctor were endless, and he couldn't knock patients back.

Back in Sydney he'd been at the cutting edge of thoracic surgery. Here, his life was so circumscribed he couldn't even watch frogs.

And he shouldn't even watch Polly.

CHAPTER SEVEN

THERE WAS A FROG, right underneath her window. Not the origami variety. The croaking sort.

She should be able to write to a Member of Parliament about that, she thought. *Dear Sir, I wish to report a breach of the peace. Surely environmental protection laws decree there shall be no noise after ten p.m....*

If she was honest, though, it wasn't the frog that was keeping her awake.

She'd given in an hour ago and taken a couple of the pills Hugo had left for her. Her aches were thus dulled. She couldn't blame her sleeplessness on them, either.

What?

This set-up. Lying in a bedroom with the window open, the smells of the bushland all around her. The total quiet—apart from the frog. Polly was a city girl. She was used to traffic, the low murmur of air conditioning and the background hum of a major metropolis.

There was no hum here. She really was in the back of beyond.

With Hugo and Ruby.

And they were both tugging at her heartstrings and she hadn't come here for her heartstrings to be tugged. She'd come here to give her heartstrings time out.

She'd had a surfeit of loving. Loving up to her eyebrows. And fuss. And emotional blackmail.

Why was it important to make a little girl happy?

Emotional blackmail?

'If I'm stuck here I might as well do my best,' she told herself. 'It's the least I can do and I always do the least I can do.'

Only she didn't. She'd been trained since birth to make people happy. This Christmas was all about getting away from that obligation.

Though she had enjoyed her origami frogs, she conceded. She had enjoyed giving Ruby pleasure.

Frogs... Origami frogs...

Real frogs...

Blurring...

Uh oh.

She was light-headed, she conceded. Just a little. Sometimes sleeplessness preceded a hypo. She should get some juice, just in case.

She padded through to the kitchen in her bare feet and the cute silk pyjamas her mum had brought her back from Paris last year.

They were a funny colour. The patterns seemed to be swirling.

That was an odd thought. Actually, all her thoughts were odd. She fetched a glass of juice and then, still acting on blurry impulse, she headed out to the veranda. If she couldn't sleep, maybe she could talk to the frog.

Hugo was sitting on the top step.

He was a dark shape against the moonlight. She would have backed away, but the screen door squeaked as she swung it open.

He turned and saw her and shifted sideways on the step, inviting her to join him.

'Problem?' he asked and she hesitated for a moment before deciding *What the heck*. She sat down. The moon was full, lighting the valley with an eerie glow. From this veranda you could see for ever.

She concentrated—very hard—on looking out over the valley rather than thinking about the man beside her.

She failed.

His body was warm beside her. Big and warm and solid.
The rest of the night...not so solid.

'Blood sugar?' he asked and she remembered she was
carrying juice. For some reason it seemed important not to
make a big deal of it. She put it down carefully behind her.

A great blond shape shifted from the dog bed behind
her. Hamster had been returned home this afternoon. Now
he was headed for her juice. She went to grab it but Hugo
was before her.

'Leave,' he ordered, in a voice that brooked no argument,
and Hamster sighed and backed away. Hugo handed Polly
back her juice—and their fingers touched.

It was a slight touch. Very slight. There was no reason
why the touch should make her shiver.

She was...shivery.

It was warm. Why was she shivering?

'Polly?'

'Wh...what?'

'Blood sugar. You're carrying juice. I assume that's why
you're up. Have you checked?'

'N...no.'

'Where's your glucose meter?'

'I'm okay.'

'Polly...'

'Don't fuss. I hate f...fussing.' But, even as she said it, she
realised there was a reason. She was still fuzzy. Too fuzzy.
Damn, she was good at predicting hypos. Where had this
come from?

But Hugo was already raising her hand, propelling the
glass up, holding the juice to her lips. 'Drink,' he ordered
and he made sure she drank half the glass and then he swung
himself off the step, disappeared inside and emerged a moment later with her glucometer.

Yeah, okay. He was right and she was wrong. She sighed
and stuck out her finger. He flicked on the torch on his phone

and did a quick finger prick test, then checked the result while she kept on stoically drinking. Or tried to.

As she tried for the last mouthful her hand slipped and he caught it—and the glass.

And he kept on holding.

'Why bring this out to the veranda?' he asked as he helped her with the last mouthful. She didn't bother to answer. 'Polly? You should have drunk it at the fridge if you were feeling...'

'I wasn't feeling,' she managed. 'And I know what I should have done.'

'So why didn't you do it?'

She glowered instead of answering. This was her business. Her diabetes. Her concern.

'The snake bite will have pushed you out of whack,' he said, and she thought about that for a while as the dizziness receded and the world started to right itself. In a minute she'd get up and make herself some toast, carbohydrates to back up the juice. But not yet. For now she was going nowhere.

'Out of whack,' she said cautiously, testing her voice and relieved to find the wobble had receded. 'That's a medical term?'

'Yep. Blood sugar level, two point one. You're not safe to be alone, Dr Hargreaves.'

'I am safe,' she said with cautious dignity. 'I woke up, I felt a bit odd; I fetched the juice.'

'You have glucose by the bed?'

'I...yes.'

'Why didn't you take it?'

'You sound like my mother.'

'I sound like your doctor.'

'You're not my doctor. I'm discharged. You're my friend.'

And why did that sound a loaded term? she wondered. Friend... It sounded okay. Sort of okay.

He was sitting beside her again. His body was big. Warm. Solid.

She always felt shaky after a hypo, she thought. That was all this was.

Um…post hypo lust?

Lust? She was out of her mind. She put her empty glass down on the step beside her. Hamster took an immediate interest but Hugo was no longer interested in Hamster.

'How the hell…?' he asked, quietly but she heard strength behind his voice. Strength and anger? 'How the hell did you think you'd manage in the country as a solo practitioner when you have unstable diabetes?'

'I don't have unstable diabetes. You said yourself, it was the snake.'

'So it was. And shock and stress. And this job's full of shock and stress.'

'I'd imagine every single one of your nursing staff knows how to deal with a hypo.'

'You intended telling them you were diabetic?'

'Of course. I'm not dumb.'

'And you'd accuse them of being like your mother, too?'

'Only if they fuss.' She sighed. 'I need some…'

'Complex carbohydrates to keep you stable. Of course you do. I'll get some toast.'

'I can…'

'Dr Hargreaves, you may not be my patient but I believe I'm still your boss. Keep still, shut up and conserve energy. Hamster, keep watch on the lady. Don't let her go anywhere.'

Hamster had just finished licking the inside of the juice glass, as far in as he could reach. He looked up, yawned and flopped sideways, as if he'd suddenly used up every bit of his energy.

That was a bit how she felt, Polly conceded. Having someone else make her toast was…well, it wasn't exactly standing on her own feet but it was okay.

Especially as it was Hugo.

There she was again, doing the lust thing, she thought.

The hypo must have been worse than she'd thought. She was feeling weird.

And Hugo seemed to sense it. He put a hand up and traced her cheekbone, an echo of the way she'd traced his cheek the night before. It was surely a gesture of concern, she thought, and why it had the power to make her want more...

'Sit,' he said. 'Stay. Toast.'

And she could do nothing but obey.

'Woof,' she ventured and he patted her head.

'Good girl. If you're really good I'll bring you a dog biscuit on the side.'

She ate her toast, sharing a crust or two with Hamster. Hugo made some for himself as well and they ate in silence. The silence wasn't uncomfortable, though. It was sort of...all right.

It was three in the morning. She should go back to bed. Instead, she was sitting on the veranda of a strange house in a strange place with a strange man...

He wasn't strange. He was Hugo.

Part of her—the dumb part—felt as if she'd known him all her life.

The sensible part knew nothing.

'So tell me more about you and Ruby,' she ventured into the stillness. The toast was gone. Hugo should be in bed too, she thought, but for now he seemed as content as she was just to sit. 'And you. Why are you here?'

'Do you remember me talking to you last night?'

'Yes.'

'Then you know I came back when my sister died.'

'So who was the doctor here before? After your Dad died?'

'Doc Farr. He retired here from Melbourne, thinking it was a quiet life. Ha. He intended to set up a vineyard, so he didn't want this house—my mother stayed living here. But Harry Farr felt trapped. When Mum and Grace died and I came home for good you couldn't see him for dust. I've never seen anyone leave so fast. His vineyard's still on the

market but he was so inundated with work all he wanted
was to get out of here.'

'You were working in Sydney. As a family doctor?'

'As a surgeon,' he said brusquely, as if it didn't matter.

'A surgeon.' She stared at him, stunned. 'Where?'

'Sydney Central.'

'Specialising?'

'Thoracic surgery. It doesn't matter now.'

'You left thoracic surgery to come here?' She was still
staring. 'Your life... Your colleagues... Did you have a girlfriend?'

'Yes, but...'

'But she wouldn't come. Of course she wouldn't.'

'Polly, I don't need to tell...'

'You don't need to tell me anything,' she said hastily. 'I'm
sorry. But Sydney... Friends? Surfing? Restaurants? The
whole social scene of Sydney?'

'It doesn't matter!'

'I suspect it does matter. A lot. You had to leave everything to take care of Ruby. That's the pits.'

'It's no use thinking it's the pits. It's just...what it is. Ruby
would know no one in Sydney, and if I stayed in my job she'd
never see me. She needs me. She's my family.'

And there was nothing to say to that.

Family... The thing she most wanted to escape from.

She thought about it as the warmth and stillness enveloped them. It was a weirdly intimate setting. A night for
telling all?

Hugo had bared so much. There were things unspoken,
things that didn't need to be spoken. He was trapped, more
than she'd ever been trapped. By Ruby... A needy seven-
year-old.

'Tell me about the Christmas thing,' she ventured, and
he started, as if his mind had been a thousand miles away.

'Christmas?'

'Why is it so important?'

'I guess it's not,' he said heavily. 'Except I promised. Actually, Grace promised her last year. She said they'd go to the beach for Christmas and then...well, I told you what happened. This year Ruby came out and asked— "Can we have a beach Christmas?" What was I supposed to say? I booked an apartment at Bondi and then spent three months advertising for a locum.'

'And bombed out with me.'

'There's no bombed about it. You saved me.'

'And you saved me right back, so we're quits.' She took a deep breath. 'Right. Christmas at the beach is important. Hugo, you can still go. Today's only Wednesday. Christmas is Saturday. You haven't cancelled, have you?'

He gave a wry laugh. 'An apartment at Bondi Beach for Christmas? I prepaid. Non-refundable. Somewhere in Bondi there's a two-bedroom flat with our name on it.'

'So go.'

'And leave you here?'

'What's wrong with leaving me here?'

'Are you kidding? Look at you.'

'I'm twenty-four hours post snake bite. It's three days until Christmas. Two more days and I'll be perky as anything.'

'You're an unstable diabetic.'

'I'm a very stable, very sensible diabetic who just happens to have been bitten by a snake. You told me yourself that the venom will have messed with things and you're absolutely right. Usually my control's awesome.'

'Awesome?'

'Well, mostly awesome,' she confessed. 'After the third margarita it can get wobbly.'

'You have to be kidding. Margaritas!'

'One margarita contains alcohol, which tends to bring my levels down, and sugar, which brings them up. It's a fine line which I've taken years to calibrate. I'll admit after the third my calibration may get blurry, but you needn't worry. I only ever tackle a third when I have a responsible medical colleague on hand with margarita tackling equipment at the ready. So for now I've left my sombrero in Sydney. I'm anticipating a nice and sober Christmas, with not a margarita in sight.'

He was looking a bit...stunned. 'Yet you still brought your Christmas tree,' he managed.

'Christmas trees don't affect blood sugars. Don't they teach surgeons anything?'

He choked on a chuckle, and she grinned. He had the loveliest chuckle, she thought, and she felt a bit light-headed again and wondered if she could use a bit more juice but the light-headedness wasn't the variety she'd felt before. This was new. Strange...

Sitting beside this guy on the back step in the small hours was strange. Watching the moon over the valley...

The step was a bit too narrow. Hamster had wedged himself beside her—something about toast—and she'd had to edge a bit closer to Hugo.

Close enough to touch.

Definitely light-headed...

'So tell me why you're not in Sydney?' Hugo asked and she had to haul herself away from the slightly tipsy sensation of sensual pleasure and think of a nice sober answer.

'Smothering,' she said and she thought as she said it, *why?* She never talked of her background. She'd hardly confessed her claustrophobia to anyone.

He didn't push, at least not for a while. He really was the most restful person, she thought. He was just...solid. Nice.

Um...down, she told her hormones, and she edged a little way away. But not very far. An inch or more.

She could change steps. Move right away.

The idea was unthinkable.

'You want to elaborate?' he asked at last and she wondered if she did, but this night was built for intimacy and suddenly there seemed no reason not to tell him.

'My parents love me to bits,' she said. 'They married late,

I'm their only child and they adore me. To Mum, I'm like a doll, to be played with, dressed up, displayed.'

'Hence the Pollyanna...'

'You got it. Pollyanna was her favourite movie, her favourite doll and then, finally, her living, breathing version of the same. That's me. Dad's not quite so over the top, but he's pretty protective. They've always had nannies to do the hard work but there's no doubting they love me. I was diagnosed with diabetes when I was six and they were shattered. I'd been smothered with care before that. Afterwards it got out of control.'

'So don't tell me...you ran away to the circus?'

'I would have loved to,' she said simply. 'But there's a problem. I love them back.'

'That is a problem,' he said, softly now, as if speaking only to himself. 'The chains of loving...'

'They get you every which way,' she agreed. 'You and Ruby...I can see that. Anyway, I seem to have been fighting for all my life to be...me. They adore me, they want to show me off to their friends and, above all, they want to keep me safe. The fight I had to be allowed to do medicine... To them, medicine seems appallingly risky—all these nasty germs—but we're pretty much over that.'

'Good for you.'

She grimaced. 'Yeah, some things are worth fighting for, but you win one battle and there's always another. Two years ago, I started going out with the son of their best friends. Marcus was kind, eligible and incredibly socially acceptable. But...*kind* was the key word. He wanted to keep me safe, just as my parents did. I felt smothered but they were all so approving. I came within a hair's breadth of marrying him. He asked, and I might have said yes, but then I saw a video camera set up to the side and I recognised it. So, instead of falling into his arms, I found myself asking whether Dad had loaned him the camera and of course he had, and I pushed him further and he told me Mum had told him what kind of ring I'd like, and his parents knew and they were all having dinner together at that very moment and we could go tell them straight away.'

'Whoa...'

'You get it,' she said approvingly. 'They didn't. But I didn't just say "no" and run. Even then I had to let them down slowly. I pretended to get a text on my phone, an urgent re-call to the hospital, and Marcus offered to drive me and I told him to go have dinner with the parents and then I went to a bar and risked having a very bad hypo. That was when I figured I needed to sort my life. I told them all kindly, in my own way, but since then... I've fought to take control. I need to back away.'

'Which is why you're here? Doing locums?'

'Exactly,' she said with satisfaction. 'It's five whole hours' drive from my parents' Christmas. Oh, don't get me wrong, I love Christmas, but they'll all be there, at the most exclusive restaurant overlooking the harbour, all my parents' friends, though not Marcus this year because he had the decency to accept a posting to New York. He's now going out with an artist who paints abstract nudes. He's much happier than he was with me, and his parents are ap-palled. Hooray for Marcus. But the rest of them... Mum will be trying to figure who I can marry now. She's indefatiga-ble, my mum. Knock her back and she bounces back again, bounce, bounce, bounce. The rest of them will be smiling indulgently in the background, but feeling slightly sorry for Mum because she has an imperfect daughter.'

'Imperfect...?'

'Perfection has perfect teeth and skin, a toned body and designer clothes. Perfect doesn't argue, she moves in the right circles, she marries the right man and never, ever has diabetes. So here I am and I'm here to stay, so you and Ruby might as well go to Bondi because I'm a very good doctor and you've contracted me to work for two weeks and that's just what I'll do.'

'Polly...'

'Go,' she said. 'Enough of this guilt stuff. If I have this right, you've left a perfectly good career, I suspect a perfectly satisfactory girlfriend, a perfectly acceptable lifestyle, all because you love Ruby. That's some chains of loving.'

'And you've left a perfectly good career, a perfectly satisfactory boyfriend, a perfectly luxurious lifestyle all because you want to cut the chains of loving?'

'Exactly,' she said.

'So why encourage me to break away?'

'Because if you stay I'll feel guilty and I'm over guilt. Go.'

'I don't think I can.'

'Hugo,' she said, figuring a girl had to make a stand some time and it might as well be now. She was full of toast. Her blood sugars had settled nicely. She was back in control again—sort of. 'This is nuts. You're a surgeon, and a thoracic surgeon at that. I'm trained in Emergency Medicine. If a kid comes in with whooping cough, who'd be most qualified to cope?'

'Whooping cough's lung...'

'Okay, bad example. Itch. In he comes, scratch, scratch, scratch. Is it an allergy or is it fleas? What's the differential appearance? Or could it be chickenpox? Some kids don't get immunised. And if it's chickenpox, what's the immunisation period? Then the next kid comes in, sixteen years old, cramps. How do you get information out of a sullen teenager? Do you suspect pregnancy?'

'Not if it's a boy. Is this an exam?'

'Do you know the answers?'

'I've been working as a family doctor for twelve months now.'

'And I've been training as an emergency doctor for five years. I win.'

'Did you know you look extraordinarily cute in those pyjamas?'

'Did you know you look extraordinarily sexy in those

jeans? Both of which comments are sexist, both beneath us as medical professionals and neither taking this argument forward. If you can't come up with a better medical rebuttal then I win.'

'You can't.'

'I just have. Give me one more day to get my bearings and you leave on Thursday.'

'Friday,' he said, sounding goaded. 'Tomorrow's another rest day and I spend Thursday watching you work.'

'That's ridiculous, plus it's discriminatory. I have diabetes, not gaps in my medical training. Tell you what, for the next two days we work side by side. That'll give you time with Ruby and it should set your mind at rest. If at the end of Thursday you can truthfully say I'm a bad doctor then I'll leave.'

'Go back to Sydney?'

'That's none of your business.'

'No,' he said. 'It's not. Polly, it's not safe.'

'Go jump. Ruby's Christmas is at stake. You're leaving, I'm staying, Dr Denver, and that's all there is to it. I have a nice little Christmas pudding for one in my suitcase, and I'm not sharing. Go away.'

'I can't.'

'You have no choice. Ruby needs you.'

'Everyone needs me,' he said, sounding even more goaded.

'I don't need you,' she retorted. 'I don't need you one bit. So get used to it, and while you're getting used to it, you might like to pack and leave.'

CHAPTER EIGHT

HIS STIPULATION WAS that Polly stayed in bed until noon. She agreed, but reluctantly. She also didn't like it that Hugo had pulled in yet more help.

His housekeeper was away. Ruby was on school holidays. He needed to care for Ruby, but Polly figured she could at least do that.

But she'd got tired of arguing last night. She'd fallen back into bed and when she woke it was nine o'clock. Okay, Hugo had a point. As a childminder she was currently less than efficient.

She snagged her glucose meter and took a reading. Six point three. *Nice.* 'I've won, Snake,' she said out loud and settled back on her pillows feeling smug.

Or sort of smug. She was still sore. She'd made origami gifts with Ruby the day before, but in truth it had been a struggle. Maybe Hugo was right with his two days of rest.

He looked like a man who was used to being right, she thought. Typical surgeon.

But the thought didn't quite come off in her head. It sounded a bit...lame.

Hugo wasn't typical anything, she thought.

There was a scratch on the door.

'Yes?'

Ruby's head poked around. Looking scared. She'd relaxed a little the day before when she'd been engrossed in origami frogs, but tension was never far from this little one.

'Hi.' Polly smiled, hoping for a smile in return.

'Are you awake?' she whispered.

'Yes.' She edged over on the bed. 'Want to come and visit?' The bedspread was pretty—patchwork. Had Ruby's grandma made it?

The house was cosy. A family house. Home of Hugo and Grace and their mum and dad.

She found herself hoping Grace had had a happy childhood and suddenly she thought she bet she had. Depression usually didn't strike until the teens. She looked out of the window at the valley beyond. A tyre swing was hanging from a huge gum nearer to the house.

Hugo would have used that swing…

She was still feeling odd. How bad had that hypo been last night? She shouldn't be feeling weird now.

Ruby was still by the door, still looking nervous, but she was obviously on a mission. 'I have to find out your blood sugar level before you get up,' Ruby quavered and Polly pulled herself back to the here and now.

Blood sugar level. It was six point three; she'd just taken it. She went to say it but then she paused. Something made her stop.

I have to find out your blood sugar level…

'Did your Uncle Hugo tell you to find out?'

'He says you're d…diabetic and your blood sugar has to be under ten and above four and if it's not I have to ring him and he says I have to make sure you still have juice on your bedside table.'

Polly glanced at her bedside table. There was a glass of juice there.

Hugo must have brought it in last night or early this morning. He must have come into her bedroom while she was asleep.

Creepy?

No. Caring.

But she didn't like caring. She didn't like fuss. She'd been swamped with fuss since childhood.

Ruby was patiently waiting for an answer.

'Can you help me with my glucose meter?' she asked and motioned to the small machine beside her.

'What does it do?'

'If you hold it out, I put my finger in it and it takes a tiny pinprick of blood. It tests the blood and gives a reading.'

'Does it hurt?'

'Not if you hold it still.'

Ruby looked fascinated. Still a bit scared, though. 'I don't want to hurt you.'

'I can do it myself,' Polly confessed. 'But I have to be brave, and now I have a sore hand. It would help if you do it for me.'

And Ruby tilted her chin and took a deep breath. 'Like doctors do?'

'Exactly.'

'My Uncle Hugo is a doctor.'

'Yes.'

'He could do it.'

'Yes, but he's not here. It's lucky I have you.'

'Yes,' Ruby said seriously and picked up the glucose meter and studied it. She turned it over and figured it out.

'That's the on switch?'

'Yes.'

'Then I think you have to put your finger in here.'

'Yes.'

'Do we have to wash your finger first?'

'You're practically a real doctor,' Polly said with admiration. 'Wow, how do you know that? Ruby, I would disinfect my finger if this wasn't my meter, but I'm the only person ever to use this. There are only my germs in there. I take a chance.'

Ruby raised one sceptical eyebrow. 'But it'd be safer if I did wash your finger,' she declared and who was Polly to argue?

'Yes,' she conceded, and Ruby gave a satisfied nod and

fetched a damp facecloth and a towel and a tube of disinfectant.

She proceeded to wipe Polly's finger, dry it and then apply disinfectant cream. A lot of disinfectant cream.

'Now it's done its job, maybe we need to use a tissue to wipe most of it off,' Polly offered. 'Otherwise, we'll be testing the disinfectant instead of my blood. You'd be able to tell your Uncle Hugo that your tube of disinfectant is safe, but not me.'

And Ruby stared down at the ooze of disinfectant, she looked at the meter—and she giggled.

It was a good giggle. A child's giggle, and Polly guessed, just by looking at her, that for this child giggles were few and far between. But the giggle died. Ruby was back in doctor mode. She fetched a tissue and wiped the finger with all the gravitas in the world.

'Put your finger in,' she ordered Polly, and Polly put her finger in and the machine clicked to register the prick and seconds later the reading came out.

'Six point eight,' Ruby said triumphantly. 'That's good.'

'That's excellent,' came a gruff voice behind them and Ruby whirled round and Polly looked up and Hugo was standing in the doorway.

How long had he been there? How much had he heard?

He was smiling. *Oh, that smile...*

'That's really good,' he reiterated and he crossed to the bed and ruffled Ruby's pigtailed hair. Which was easy to do because the pigtails looked very amateurish—blonde wisps were escaping every which way. 'Thank you, Ruby. How's our patient? Was she brave when you did the finger prick?'

'Yes,' Ruby said. 'She moved a little bit when it went in, but she didn't scream.'

'I didn't,' Polly said, adding a touch of smug to her voice. 'I'm very brave.'

'It's all about how you hold the meter.' Hugo was talking to Ruby, not her. 'You must have very steady hands.'

'Yes,' the little girl said, and smiled shyly up at her uncle but there was anxiety behind the smile. 'I did. Are we really still going to the beach for Christmas?'

'We're going to try,' Hugo told her. 'I told you this morning, and I mean it. If we can get Dr Hargreaves better...'

'I'm Polly,' Polly said fast, because it seemed important.

'If we can look after Polly,' Hugo corrected himself. 'If we can make her better, then she can be the doctor and we can still have our holiday.'

'She doesn't look like a doctor,' Ruby said dubiously.

'She doesn't, does she? Those are very pretty pyjamas she's wearing.'

'They are,' Ruby conceded. He and Ruby were examining her as if she were some sort of interesting bug. 'I'd like pyjamas like that.'

'I think I can find some like these on the Internet in your size,' Polly ventured. 'If it's okay with your uncle.'

'Doctors don't wear pyjamas.' Ruby seemed distracted by Polly's offer but not enough to be deflected from her main purpose, which was obviously to find out exactly how qualified Polly was to take over here and thus send Ruby to the beach.

'Does your uncle have a white coat?' Polly demanded, and Ruby nodded.

'He has lots. They're hanging in the airing cupboard.'

'If you put one of those on me, I'll look just like a doctor.'

'But your hair's too red,' Ruby told her. 'Doctors don't have red curly hair.'

'You've been moving with the wrong type of doctor. The best doctors all have red curly hair. If the medical board discovered your Uncle Hugo's hair was black and almost straight he'd be sent to the nearest hairdresser to buy a wig.'

'A wig...' Ruby's eyes widened.

'You can get wigs on the Internet too. You want to help me look?'

'No!' Hugo said, and both girls turned and stared at him.

At his hair. It was thick and short. It only just qualified as wavy—definitely not curly—and it was definitely black.

'A red wig would be perfect,' Polly decreed, and Ruby giggled and giggled some more and Hugo's face creased into a grin and Polly lay back on her pillows and smug didn't begin to describe how she was feeling.

She'd been in some tight situations before this. Lots of tight situations. As an emergency physician she'd even saved lives. It had felt great, but somehow this moment was right up there. Making Hugo and his niece smile.

'Ruby, Mrs Connor's just asked if you'd like to go to the pictures in Willaura,' Hugo said, almost nonchalantly. 'Three girls from your class will be there. Talia and Sasha and Julie. Mr Connor will pick you up in ten minutes if you want to go.'

And he picked up the glucose meter and studied it as if it was really interesting instead of something doctors saw all the time—and Polly realised that this was important.

How many times did Ruby accept this kind of invitation? She suspected seldom. Or never?

'Don't I have to look after Polly?' Ruby asked dubiously.

'She's awake now and she's been tested and her blood sugar's good. We'll give her breakfast and then she needs to go back to sleep. We can ask Hamster to snooze under her bed to look after her.'

'We could put a white coat on Hamster,' Ruby said and giggled again. 'He could be the doctor. And I could maybe teach the girls how to make frogs.'

'That's a grand plan,' Hugo told her and Ruby swooped off to get ready.

And Hugo was left with Polly and Polly was left with Hugo and suddenly there were no words.

What was it with this woman?

What was it that made him want to smile?

She should be just another patient, he told himself, or just another colleague.

She was both. She was neither.

She lay in the too big bed in her cute swirly pyjamas, pink and orange and crimson and purple. They should have clashed with her red hair but they didn't. She looked up at him and she was still smiling but her smile was tentative. A bit uncertain.

She looked...vulnerable, he thought, and suddenly he realised that was how he was feeling.

Vulnerable. As if this woman was somehow edging under his defences.

He didn't have defences. What sort of stupid thought was that?

'Lorna will bring you breakfast,' he told her.

'Lorna?'

'My housekeeper for this morning. Our usual housekeeper, Lois, has taken Christmas off.'

'And because of me you're having to find fill-ins.'

'I told you. Yes, because of you, Ruby and I are stuck here, but if it wasn't for you I wouldn't be here in the worst sense of the term. So lie back and get better without qualms. What would you like for breakfast?'

'Toast and marmalade,' she said, almost defiantly, and he raised an eyebrow in exactly the same way she'd just seen Ruby do it.

'Don't tell me.' The corner of his mouth quirked upward. 'Plus coffee with three sugars.'

'If you're about to lecture me...'

He held up his hands as if to ward off attack. 'You're a big girl, Dr Hargreaves. You manage your own diabetes. And we do have sourdough, which has a low...'

'Glycaemic index. I know.' She glowered. 'If you turn into my mother I'm out of here.'

'For the next two days I'm your doctor and I have a vested interest in getting your diabetes stable.'

'I like sugar.'

'You had enough last night to keep you going for a week.'

And she knew he was right, he thought. Her protests were almost instinctive—the cry of a kid who'd been protected since diagnosis, told what to eat and when, who'd not been given a chance to make her own choices.

'I'm not silly and I'm not a child,' she muttered, confirming what he'd thought.

'I know you're not. And of course you can have marmalade.'

'Your generosity overwhelms me.'

'Good,' he said cheerfully. 'Let me look at your hand.'

She held it out for inspection. He lifted a corner of the dressing and nodded.

'It's looking good. If you stay here and work you'll need to be extra careful. Glove up for everything.'

'Yes, Grandpa.'

'The correct term is *Doctor*. Say, *"Yes, Doctor"*.'

'Won't,' she said and grinned, and he looked down into her face, that smattering of freckles, at those gorgeous auburn curls and…

And he had to get out of here.

She was messing with his equilibrium.

'Call Lorna if you need anything,' he said and she glowered.

'Why is Lorna staying? Ruby's going to her friends. Hamster and I are fine.'

'Humour me,' he told her. 'Lorna will stay until after lunch, just until I'm sure that you're…safe.'

'I don't like being safe,' she snapped and he grinned and patted her head as if he was patting Ruby's head.

Except it wasn't like that at all. It felt…different. Intimate. *Okay?*

'Says the woman who's just been playing with snakes,' he told her. 'You don't like being safe? You know, Dr Hargreaves, I'm very sure that you do.'

Polly slept on and off for the rest of the day. She woke late afternoon and looked at the time and nearly had kittens. Five o'clock? Where had the day gone? She must have been more shocked than she'd realised.

Lorna had brought in sandwiches around midday. She'd eaten two. The other plus her untouched mug of coffee still sat on her bedside table.

Two days' rest. 'That's enough,' she told herself and headed across to the bathroom and showered—just a little grateful for the hand rail—and then tugged on jeans and a T-shirt and pulled a comb through her curls.

Hamster was still under her bed. The rest of the house was in silence.

She ate her remaining sandwiches—yeah, she did have to be careful—checked her blood sugars and felt smug again and then headed to the kitchen.

No one.

There was a note from Lorna on the kitchen table.

I've had to go, Dr Hargreaves, but Dr Denver thinks you'll be okay. My number's on the pad by the phone if you need me. Ruby's staying at Talia's for a sleepover. Dr Denver has some emergency over at the hospital. He says help yourself to what you need and he'll see you as soon as he can. Fridge is full. Good luck.

She hardly needed good luck. She opened the fridge and stared in and thought it would take a small army to eat their way through this.

She meandered through the empty house feeling a bit intrusive, a bit weird. It was still very much Hugo's parents' home, she thought, furnished and decorated over years of raising a family. There were pictures of Hugo and a girl who was evidently Grace as babies, as they grew up. There were pictures of high school graduations, Hugo's medical graduation. Happy snaps.

Though Polly could see the telltale signs of early depression on Grace's face as soon as she reached her teens. Hugo smiled obediently at the camera. Some of his smiles said he was long-suffering but Grace's smiles seemed forced.

As were the smiles Grace produced in later photos, taken with Ruby.

Depression… *Aagh.* It was a grey fog, thick sludge, permeating everything and destroying lives.

And now it had destroyed Hugo's.

But had it been destroyed? He'd had to leave Sydney, commit himself to his family.

It'd be the same if Polly had to stay in Sydney, commit herself to her family.

'He has the bigger load to bear,' Polly said out loud, though then she thought of Hugo ruffling Ruby's hair and saw there would be compensations. And this did seem like an awesome place to live.

'But people probably think that about the six-star places my parents want to cocoon me in,' she muttered and thought: *enough.*

What she needed was work. Or at least an introduction to work.

She thought back to the note:

Dr Denver has some emergency over at the hospital…

Work. *Excellent.*

She found one of Hugo's white coats. It was a bit too big—okay, it was a lot too big, but with the sleeves rolled up she decided she looked almost professional.

'See you later,' she told Hamster but Hamster heaved himself to his feet and padded determinedly after her.

'Are you my minder?' she demanded and he wagged his tail and stuck close.

'Has he told you to bite me if I'm not sensible?'

Hamster wagged some more and she sighed and gave up and headed across to the hospital, her minder heading after her.

CHAPTER NINE

SURGEONS WEREN'T TRAINED to cope with human conflict. Surgeons operated.

Yes, surgeons consulted pre-operatively. Yes, they visited their patients at their bedsides, but consultations were done within the confines of appointments, and patient visits were made with a nurse hovering close by, ready to whisk away all but the closest of friends or family.

Death, however, observed no such restrictions. Max Hurley had passed away peacefully in his sleep, aged ninety-seven. He'd been in the nursing home section of the hospital for the last twelve months, during which time his daughter Isobel had been a constant visitor, having nursed him at home for years. His wife had died ten years back. Hugo had assumed there was little other family.

Two hours after his death, he'd learned how wrong he was. A vast extended family had descended on the place like a swarm of locusts. Isobel, seventy years old and frail herself, was jammed into a chair at the edge of the room while her family railed around her.

One of the older men in the group looked almost ready to have a medical incident himself. He was red in the face and the veins on his forehead were bulging. 'I can't believe it!' he was shouting. 'He's left her the whole blasted farm. She's seventy. A spinster. What the hell…? It's a family farm. It's hard up against my place. The old man always intended the farms to be joined. We'll be contesting…'

'There's no need!' another man snapped. 'Isobel will be reasonable, won't you, Isobel?' The men were standing over

her, obviously furious. 'But, as for your farms being joined...
We'll split, fair down the middle. You get half, Bert, and I'll
get the other half. Isobel, we can organise you a nice little
retirement unit in town...'

Isobel was surrounded by her family, but what a family!
She had a buxom woman sitting on either side of her. One
was even hugging her, but she looked...

Small. He could think of no better adjective. Her father's
death seemed to have shrunk her.

Any man's death diminishes me... It was a quote from
John Donne and, looking down at the helpless Isobel, he
thought, even though her dad had been almost a hundred,
that diminishment was just as powerful.

'Do you want everyone to leave?' he asked Isobel, thinking she needed time to be alone with her father, but she
shook her head.

'N...no. These are my family.'

Family. This was her call, but oh, he felt for her. Trapped
by loving...

But then, suddenly, standing at the door was Polly. Her
white coat reached her knees, with the sleeves rolled up two
or three times. Her freckles stood out in her still pale face,
accentuating the flame of her curls, but her green eyes were
flashing professionalism—and determination.

She was wearing a stethoscope around her neck. A red
one. It was inscribed, he thought, fascinated. *What the
heck...?*

Who had a personally inscribed stethoscope?

'I'm sorry but I need you all to leave,' she said and he
stopped thinking about personalised stethoscopes and stared
at her in amazement.

He'd thought of her as small, frail, ill.

She sounded like a boom box with the volume turned
up full.

'I'm Dr Hargreaves and I'm here to organise the death
certificate,' she said so loudly that she cut across arguments,

squashing the gathering that was threatening to become a riot. 'Dr Denver has asked me to confirm his diagnosis and I have limited time. I need the immediate next of kin. Who's that?'

After a moment's stunned silence Isobel put up a timid hand.

Polly nodded. 'You can stay. Everyone else must leave.'

'Why?' the oldest of the arguing men demanded. 'What the...?'

'If you wish to avoid a coroner's inquest and possible autopsy then this is what has to happen.' Polly glanced at her watch. 'My time is precious. Could you leave now?'

'You're the doc who got bitten by a snake.'

'Yes, which has pushed my workload to crazy limits before Dr Denver leaves on vacation. Go now, please, or I'll be forced to request an independent assessment from Sydney.'

'When can we come back?'

'When I've made my assessment and, since I've never treated this patient, it may be a while. I suggest...' She hesitated and looked at Isobel, and then at Hugo.

'This is Isobel,' Hugo told her, starting to enjoy himself.

'I suggest Isobel will tell you when it's possible,' Polly continued smoothly. 'Meanwhile, my apologies for the inconvenience but you have two minutes to say your goodbyes before I must start work.'

'We're family,' the closest guy muttered and Polly nodded.

'I can see that, and my condolences, but I'm afraid Isobel needs to face this alone.'

And then she stood back and crossed her arms and waited.

She was superb, Hugo thought. If he didn't know she was talking nonsense—in truth he'd already signed the death certificate—he'd have been totally taken in.

'Why do you need to worry about a death certificate?' one of the men demanded. 'He just died of old age.'

'That's nonsense,' Polly snapped. 'How old are you?'

'I...seventy-two.' There was something about Polly that said *Don't mess with me*, and the guy clearly got it.

'So you're older than your prescribed three score years and ten. If you drop dead now, surely you'd expect us to dignify your death with a diagnosis. Not just dismiss it as old age.'

'Yes, but...'

'But what? Do extra years mean fewer rights, less respect?'

'No, but...'

'Then please leave and let me get on with my work.' And, to Hugo's further astonishment, she stared at her watch and started toe tapping. Less than one minute later the room was clear and the door closed behind them.

As the door closed Isobel gave a muffled sob and crossed to the bed and hugged her father.

How had Polly understood this? Hugo thought, stunned. How had she figured so fast that Isobel desperately needed time alone? That sometimes family wasn't wanted.

'We'll come back in an hour,' he said gently and touched Isobel's shoulder. 'Or earlier, if you want. The bell's here. Just press it if you need it.'

Isobel's tear-stained face turned up to them. 'Thank you. I didn't think... When I got the call to say he was going I rang Henry to ask him to feed the dogs and suddenly they were all here. I didn't even know they knew the contents of the will. And...'

'And it doesn't matter,' Hugo said gently. 'All those things can be sorted later. I think it'd be a good idea if we got Ron Dawson—he's your dad's lawyer, isn't he?—to take responsibility for any questions. If anyone asks, just say Ron's in charge. No more questions, Isobel. No more worry. For now it's simply time to say goodbye to your dad.'

And he ushered Polly out of the room and closed the door behind them.

Wherever Isobel's obnoxious family were, they were no longer here. The silence after the din was almost tangible.

Joe came round the corner from the nurses' station, his arms above his head in a gesture of triumph. 'You're a champ, Doc Hargreaves,' he boomed. 'A clean knockout. You can come and work here any day.'

'Did you set that up?' Hugo asked faintly and Joe grinned.

'All I did was tell Polly that you and Isobel were surrounded by a rabid pack of mercenary relatives and she went off like a firecracker. I listened from out in the corridor. Did you ever hear anything like it? A couple of them asked how long before they could go back in and I said our Doc Hargreaves is known for thorough work. A detailed examination, pathology, maybe even scans. It could take until tomorrow.'

'Scans...' Hugo managed and Polly grinned happily up at Joe and Joe high-fived her with her good hand and suddenly Hugo was left feeling a bit...

Jealous? Jealous of his fifty-year-old head nurse high-fiving his colleague? He had to be kidding.

'Of course, scans,' Polly said happily. 'You have to scan a patient very thoroughly when you're looking for cause of death.' She tugged up her jeans and held up her still swollen foot. 'If you hadn't scanned me you might have missed the snake bite. See? Two little holes. Scans are vital and they can take as much time as Isobel needs.'

Hugo choked. Joe guffawed and high-fived Polly again then a bell rang down the corridor and Joe took himself off and Hugo was left with Polly.

She was amazing.

She was gorgeous!

'So,' she said, turning brisk again. 'Are you going to show me your hospital?' And she was back to being a colleague, purely professional, except her coat was too big and her hair was too red and her toenails were crimson and...

And she was a colleague.

'Sure,' he said and managed to do a decent professional

tour of his hospital without once—or maybe once but that was professional, as she bumped her leg on a trolley and he had to make sure the swollen ankle was still okay—looking at those amazing toenails.

And she was terrific. Any doubts he might have had about her ability to care for the medical needs of Wombat Valley were put to rest fast. She was just…right.

He now had four patients in his nursing home beds—yes, Max had just died, but over the last twenty-four hours he'd had two new admissions. Christmas often did that. The family was heading away for the holiday, Dad couldn't cope on his own and the easiest solution was respite care. Or a lonely senior citizen was suddenly overwhelmed with the memories of Christmases past and got chest pain or stopped eating, or even forgot normal care and fell…

Hazel Blacksmith was one such lady. She'd fallen chopping her firewood last night. Her hip had proven to be badly bruised rather than broken but she lay in bed, a ball of misery, refusing to be comforted.

But Polly didn't acknowledge misery. 'Hey, how lucky are you?' Polly demanded as Hugo introduced her and explained the diagnosis. 'Just a bruised hip? If someone made me chop wood I'd probably end up suffering from amputation from the knee down.'

'I've chopped wood all me life,' Hazel told her in a firmer voice than Hugo had heard since her neighbour had brought her in. 'I don't cut meself.'

'And you don't get bitten by snakes either, I'll bet,' Polly said. 'Wise woman. Look at this.' And she stuck her leg in the air for Hazel to see her snake bite.

'I heard you got bit,' Hazel said cautiously.

'It was Dr Denver's fault.' Polly cast a darkling look at Hugo. 'He trapped the snake with his shenanigans in the truck, so when I went to rescue them it was ready to attack.'

And Hazel's lips twitched. 'Shenanigans…'

'Men,' Polly said. 'You can't trust them to do anything

right. Holding snakes by the tail is the least of it. Would you mind if I had a look at your bruise? I've much gentler hands than Dr Denver.'

They were gentle. Hugo watched as Polly performed a careful examination of the old lady—a scan? She gently probed and teased and by the end of the examination the old lady was smitten and Hugo was getting close himself.

What a gem! He would be able to go away for Christmas and leave the hospital in her charge.

But...why did going away for Christmas suddenly not seem as desirable?

'Are you staying in for Christmas?' Polly asked cheerfully as she tucked Hazel's bedclothes back around her and Hazel looked brighter than she had since Hugo had admitted her.

'Dr Denver thinks I should.'

'Then I concur,' Polly said warmly. 'But I need to warn you, the Christmas dinner menu here is looking a bit dodgy. However, we have three more days. I'll see what I can do. I'll ring my mother's chef and get some advice.'

'Your mother has a chef?' Hazel sounded stunned.

And Hugo was stunned as well. Not only did this woman come from a privileged background, she was happily admitting it.

'Doesn't everyone's mother?' Polly said happily. 'Left to my own devices, I'm a beans on toast girl, but this is Christmas. We all have to make some sacrifices, and ringing Raoul might be the least of them. Just as long as he promises not to tell my mother where I am.'

She wasn't making sacrifices at all, Polly thought happily as she sat on the veranda that evening. She was about to have a very good time.

Her ankle still hurt. Her hand ached, but not so much as to mess with her equanimity. This was a beautiful little hospital, full of easy patients, and she was pretty sure she could cope.

Her silver tree was up in the living room, surrounded by origami gifts and a few real ones as well.

Hamster was lying by her side on the top step. He was due to head back to his temporary carer's but she intended to have a word with Hugo about that. She wouldn't mind Hamster staying here for Christmas as well.

She'd do a bit of online shopping, she decided. If she paid enough for express postage, she could get heaps of good stuff here. Lots of treats for her coterie of oldies in the hospital.

Would Isobel like to come too? Maybe she could take her tree over to the hospital and have Christmas dinner over there?

Maybe she could wear her little red alpine dress and the wig with the blonde pigtails. And her crimson boots and the Santa hat. She just happened to have packed them.

She grinned. Three suitcases... A girl could never be prepared enough.

The screen door opened behind her and Hugo emerged carrying two mugs of tea. She nudged over on her step, heaving Hamster to the side as well, and he sat down beside her.

Ma and Pa Kettle, she thought, and the feeling was sort of...okay.

More than okay. Good.

She liked this man.

Actually...

Um...don't go there. He'd be gone before Christmas. He'd come back in the New Year, she'd do a quick handover and then she'd have no reason to see him again.

Her bounce faded a little as she took the offered mug and she gave herself a swift inward kick. What was she thinking? Having fantasies about a man who was so steeped in domesticity he couldn't get out of this valley?

Falling for a man who was committed to love?

Love was what she was running from, she thought dryly. Love was why she'd packed her car and headed for the hills.

Love was chains, blackmail, guilt. Love was your mother

watching every mouthful you ate and mentally counting insulin dosages. Love was catching your boyfriend phoning in to report how you were— 'She's great, Mrs Hargreaves, and of course I'm looking after her. No, of course I won't let her get tired...'

Toerag. She glowered at the absent Marcus and took her tea and stared morosely out into the dark.

'Hamster been annoying you, then?' Hugo asked mildly and she caught herself and managed a rueful smile.

'Not so much.'

'Are you hurting? How's your...?'

'Don't you dare fuss!'

'Okay,' he said cautiously.

Silence.

It wasn't bad tea. Good and hot.

It was very hard to appreciate tea when Hugo was sitting beside her.

'Where would you be now?' she asked, suddenly needing to know. 'If it wasn't for Ruby.'

'Sydney.'

Of course. 'Working?'

'Possibly. If I wasn't on call, though, I'd be in a supper club around the corner from the hospital. It has a roof top bar that overlooks the harbour. Most of my friends use it.'

'And you miss it?'

'What do you think?'

'And your work? Your surgery?'

'Almost more than I can bear,' he said and she flinched at the sudden and honest sound of gut-wrenching loss.

'So why don't you take Ruby back to Sydney?'

'If I had Ruby in Sydney, do you believe for a moment that I'd be in the supper club?'

'You could get a housekeeper.'

'Yes, I could. The problem is that I love Ruby.'

'She's prickly.'

'Tough to love. She is. She lets me, though. Inch by inch.'

'Is it worth it?'

'What, hoping for Ruby's love in return?'

'I guess,' she said, doubtfully though, because she wasn't quite sure where she was going with this.

'I don't have a choice,' Hugo said gently. 'And I can't count its worth. I met Ruby when she was two days old. My sister was in a mess. I was called to a hospital up in Darwin because Grace was drug addicted and unable to cope. She went into rehab. I took four weeks off work, then my parents took over. But for those four weeks... I held Ruby in the palm of my hands—literally—and she's been there ever since.'

And what was there in that to make her tear up? Nothing, she thought, frantically sniffing, and Hugo handed her a tissue and she thought this was just the sort of man who walked round with spare tissues in his pocket because something about him made you...made her...

Back off. She needed to back off. She'd been here for less than three days and suddenly it seemed as if a fine gossamer web was closing around her. The web she'd run from.

A trap, every bit as claustrophobic as the one Hugo found himself in.

She stood up, so suddenly she splashed tea on Hamster, who looked up reproachfully and then started licking the tea from his paws.

Hugo looked up too, but not reproachfully. It was as if he understood where she was coming from.

And that was a scary thought all by itself.

'I should go to bed,' she said a bit shakily and he nodded.

'You should.'

And then his phone rang.

He answered it, listened, then clicked it closed and rose as well.

'Work?'

'What do you think?'

'Anything I can help with?'

'You're going to bed.'

'Is that an order?'

'Um...no.'

'So tell me.'

'Groin and knee injuries,' he said. 'Terry Oakshot. Local farmer and amateur footy player. Late twenties. This sounds like a party prank gone wrong. His mates are bringing him in now.'

'I'll stay up until I see what the problem is.'

'No need. If I can't handle it I'll send him out.'

'Evacuate when you have two doctors?'

'If I need to evacuate, I'll evacuate.'

'Of course you will,' she said warmly. 'But if it's not too complicated, don't forget I'm not just a pretty face.' She grinned and took his mug. 'Okay, Doc Denver, you go see what the problem is, but yell if you need me. I'll go put my feet up and garner strength for the onslaught to come. Ooh, I wouldn't mind a good onslaught. I'm a wee bit bored.'

CHAPTER TEN

ONE LOOK AT the mess that was Terry Oakshot's knee confirmed that he needed a surgeon skilled in reconstruction. The blood supply wasn't compromised, though. There was no need for immediate intervention for his knee. He needed decent pain relief and transport as soon as possible to the experts in Sydney.

Unfortunately, it wasn't his knee that was causing Terry to whimper. He was clutching his groin in agony.

It would be agony too, Hugo thought, as Joe helped examine him.

A fast conversation with the mates who'd brought him in had given him all the information he needed. The boys had been having a pre-Christmas party in the footy ground's stadium. After a few beers someone had shouted for Terry to come down to ground level to kick the footy. After a beer or six, Terry had decided there was a faster way than the stairs and he'd tried to slide down the banister.

It hadn't been a good idea. Terry had smashed groin first into the bottom post, then toppled onto the wooden stairs. The knee was bad. His groin was worse. One side of his scrotum was swollen and cut, and one testicle was higher than the other. The less injured side didn't look too good either, and Terry was retching with pain.

'What's going on?' he moaned as his wife arrived. Maree was in her early twenties and seemed terrified. She looked as if she'd been baking. Her face was streaked white with flour, and it was whiter still with shock.

'You seem to have given yourself a testicular torsion,' he

told him. 'Terry, your knee's broken and it'll need special-ist surgery in Sydney, but what's happened to your groin is more urgent. The spermatic cord running to your testicles has been damaged. The cord's a blood vessel, so the blood supply's been cut. We need to work fast to get it sorted.'

'Fast'd be good, Doc,' Terry moaned. 'Fast like now?'

And, with that, Polly's presence came slamming back at him, bringing a wash of relief. He had an anaesthetist.

'You know I have another doctor working here?'

'The one that got bit by the snake?' Terry demanded.

'She's recovered.' Or almost recovered. She could still do with an early night but this needed to take precedence. 'Terry, you and Maree don't have any kids yet, do you?'

'No!' And Maree had understood the inference faster than Terry. 'But we want them. The spermatic cord... Doc, you're not saying...?'

'I'm thinking we need to operate fast,' Hugo told them both. 'I'll get Joe to ring Polly. She can do the anaesthetic.'

'Polly...' Maree managed. 'What sort of name is that for a doctor?'

'It's short for Pollyanna. It's a great name for a fine doc-tor,' he told her. 'Wait and see.'

Polly didn't see the wound until they were in Theatre. Terry declared he 'wasn't going to get looked at down there by a female'.

'You'll get looked at by anyone who can fix you,' Maree snapped and clutched Polly as soon as she saw her. 'We want kids,' she stammered. 'You get him right, no matter what.'

'We'll do our best,' Polly told her. She'd arrived at the hospital fast, she was heading to scrub, and she had no time to waste.

Once in Theatre she could focus, and she needed to. Terry was a big man, he was deeply shocked and he'd been drink-ing. In an ideal world she'd wait for him to sober up, but there wasn't time.

She ran through the options in her head, talked them through with Hugo. Then they went for it. With Terry safely asleep and intubated, Joe started disinfecting the injured area. For the first time she saw the extent of the damage.

'Ouch,' she said and Hugo cast her a look that could almost be amused.

'You might say that.'

But he was calm. She watched him assess the wound carefully. She watched as he started the procedure as if he'd done it a thousand times.

He was a thoracic surgeon. This was a job for a trained urologist.

He didn't look concerned. He looked...competent.

He's good, she thought, and then she relaxed a little, although not very much because her anaesthetic skills were basic, but they were good enough to spare her time to watch Hugo work.

No highly skilled urologist could do a better job than this, she thought. Repairing a damaged spermatic cord was tricky at the best of times, and that was in a large hospital with every piece of modern gadgetry. Large hospitals had magnification, monitors showing exactly what was happening. Large hospitals had skilled backup.

Hugo had a semi-trained anaesthetist, Joe and himself.

If she hadn't been here...

What then?

Hugo would have needed to send him to Sydney, she thought, and by the time Terry reached Sydney, he and his wife would be fated to be childless or needing a sperm donor.

What if this had happened when she was here by herself?

For the first time, her bold foray into bush medicine looked less than wise. She would have failed this couple.

How could Hugo work here by himself?

'If you hadn't been here I would have talked Joe through the anaesthesia. We've done it before,' Hugo said.

She glanced up at him in shock. 'How do you know what I'm thinking?'

'You have an entirely readable face. You were concentrating, concentrating, concentrating, and suddenly you looked petrified. I checked the monitors, saw you had nothing patient-wise to be petrified about and figured you had to be projecting yourself into the future.'

'He has eyes in the back of his head.' Joe was grinning. 'You'll get used to it.'

'She won't,' Hugo said. 'We'll work together tomorrow and then I'll be gone.'

But he'd be back, Polly thought as his skilled fingers continued their fight to repair the appalling damage. In the New Year he'd be back here being a solo doctor with his little niece. He'd be on his own and she'd be...

Where?

She hadn't figured that out yet. One locum at a time. Wandering...

She'd thought she'd quite like to do a stint for an aid agency, working overseas, getting right away from her parents.

Her diabetes was the killer there. No aid agency, working in Third World conditions, would accept a Type One diabetic.

Maybe that was one of the reasons she wanted it so much. Maybe the locum thing was part of it.

Locum to locum to locum? Never settling? Never doing family?

That was what she'd decided. No more fuss. She couldn't bear it.

Doing things despite her diabetes...

Was this another way her diabetes was controlling her?

'I'm thinking...' Hugo's voice was a lazy drawl but there was satisfaction behind it and it drew her attention back to where it should be. 'I'm thinking we might just have succeeded in repairing this mess. The left one's possible and the right one's looking certain. We'll transfer him to Sydney for his knee and get him checked by the urologist while he's there but I'm thinking we've done the thing.'

'Yes!' Joe said, but Polly didn't say anything at all.

Locum to locum to locum…

That was what she'd dreamed of. Why did it suddenly seem so bleak?

And why did what she'd thought of as a dream suddenly seem like running away?

There was no more time for introspection. Polly reversed the anaesthetic, Terry started to come round and Hugo sent her out to talk to Maree.

'She won't believe Joe. Something about the beard. Polly, go tell her Terry's okay.'

'So she'll believe a whippersnapper who came on the scene in polka dots with snake bite instead of a beard?' Joe demanded.

'Absolutely. If Polly, who's hung upside down with snakes, decrees someone's safe, then…'

'Then she'll think Polly has a weird definition of safe,' Joe retorted and he and Hugo chuckled and Polly looked from one to the other and thought that even though Hugo was trapped in this little hospital there were compensations.

It was like family…

Family… There was that word again.

'I have drips to adjust and you deserve to be the bearer of good tidings,' Hugo told her. 'How's the hand?'

She hadn't even noticed her hand. She'd double gloved because she couldn't scrub the dressing and then she'd forgotten about it.

Her ankle wasn't hurting. She couldn't feel a bruise.

She felt…a mile high.

Successful surgery… There was nothing like it.

She thought suddenly of her parents' recriminations when she'd decided on medicine and she knew, without doubt, that medicine at least wasn't running from her parents' world. Medicine was what she most wanted to do.

She met Hugo's gaze and he was smiling and once again she got that blast of knowledge that told her he understood what she was feeling.

'Good, isn't it?' he said softly and he smiled at her—and he might as well have kissed her.

It felt like a kiss. A caress from four feet apart.

And Joe was smiling at them, beaming from one ear to the other, and Polly stepped from the table a bit too fast and could have tripped, but she didn't. She wasn't that stupid.

She felt pretty stupid. She backed out of Theatre feeling totally discombobulated.

Terry's wife was waiting outside, sitting huddled on the room's big couch. There were people around her, two older couples who looked as if they'd come in a hurry. One of the women was wearing a crimson-smeared apron—very smeared. Her husband had matching crimson smears on his gingham shirt.

They all looked up at her as she emerged and Maree moaned and put her face in her hands.

'Hey, it's all right, love.' The bigger of the two men put a rough hand on her shoulder. He was watching Polly's face. 'The Doc's smiling. You're smiling, aren't you, Doc? You wouldn't do that if our Terry was bad.'

'I'm smiling,' Polly told them, smiling even more just to prove the point. 'Dr Denver's operated and everything went as smoothly as we could hope. Everything's been put back together. Terry's not quite recovered from the anaesthetic yet but as soon as Dr Denver's set up the drips—he'll be administering pain relief, fluids and antibiotics—you'll be able to see him.'

'Oh.' Maree put her face behind her hands and burst into tears. The crimson lady knelt down and gathered her into her arms.

'There, dear, what did I tell you? Terry always bounces

back.' And then she glared up at her husband. 'I told you. Now we have a pot full of burned toffee and a hundred un-coated toffee apples for nothing.'

There was uncertain laughter, the beginnings of relief, and then Maree put her head up again.

'And he will...we will be able to have babies?' she whis-pered.

Polly heard the door swing open behind her. She didn't have to turn to see it was Hugo—she was starting to sense this man.

Why? What was it between them?

He didn't say anything, though—it seemed this was her call.

'Maree, Dr Denver's done everything we can to make sure that can still happen. We think we've succeeded. I've just watched him operate and I don't think any city surgeon could have done better.'

'Excellent,' the toffee apple lady said. 'And will he be home for Christmas?'

'He won't be, Lexie.' And Hugo took over, putting a hand on Polly's arm as if to signal that he was about to impart medical advice from the team. It was a solid way to go, Polly thought, presenting a united front, and why it made her feel...

Um, no. She wasn't going there. Right now, she couldn't.

'Guys, we're going to send him on to Sydney,' Hugo said, firmly now. 'The operation I just performed was to his groin and, as far as I can tell, it's successful. But his knee needs a competent orthopaedic surgeon. I'd also like him checked by a specialist urologist. We'll send him on to Sydney Central as soon as possible. It'll take about an hour to get the chop-per here for transfer. Maree, if you'd like to go with him, I'll tell the hospital you'll need accommodation—they have self-contained flats for just this purpose.'

The group had been starting to relax. Now, as one, they froze.

'But it's Christmas,' Maree whispered. 'We can't go to Sydney for Christmas.'

'You don't have a choice,' Hugo said, still gently, and Maree burst into tears again.

'Hey.' The toffee apple lady still had her in her arms. 'Hey, sweetheart, it's okay. We'll manage.'

'But what about Grandma?' Maree lifted a woebegone face to Hugo. 'What about you, Mum?'

'We'll manage.'

'You can't. Grandma's got Alzheimer's,' Maree explained, looking wildly up at Hugo. 'She's so confused and she gets angry with Mum, but if Terry and I are there she calms down and Mum relaxes and enjoys Christmas. If we're not there...'

'We'll take care of things.' The other woman spoke then, a woman who by her looks had to be Terry's mum. 'We'll look after everyone.'

'But we'll be by ourselves for Christmas.'

'With a recovering husband. Surely that's the most important thing?' It was Terry's dad, glancing back at the door into Theatre, but all three women turned and glared at him.

'Christmas with family...' Maree snapped. 'What's more important than that?'

'Now you know very well that health comes first,' her mum said. 'But you know what? Terry'll be recovering. And you know Aldi Baker? She moved to her son's big house in the centre of Sydney and now her son's gone to Paris for Christmas. She's gone with him and she said if ever we want a base in Sydney we can use that house. So why not now? Why not pack all of us up and we can go to Sydney?' She looked up at Terry's parents. 'You too. Aldi says there's six bedrooms—can you believe that? It's as if it's meant. We can pick up everything—except the toffee apples—they might be well and truly stuffed and they were just for the Christmas Eve fete at the school anyway. We can take everything down there tomorrow morning. If needs be, I bet we could have Christmas in Terry's hospital room.'

'The specialists might even let him out by then,' Hugo conceded, smiling as the despair in the room turned to tentative excitement. 'He'll still need tests but if he stays in Sydney... No promises, but it's possible...'

'There you go then,' Maree's mum said and before Hugo could protect himself she'd flung her arms around him and planted what was probably a very sticky kiss on his cheek. She hugged Polly for good measure and then headed back to hug each and every one of her family.

Family...

And Polly was suddenly staring at them all thinking... *family.*

She was running away.

Why was she running?

Enough. She was tired, she decided. She was overwrought. Her emotions were all over the place. What she needed right now was bed. Hugo was right—bed rest.

Somewhere away from Hugo.

Why did the presence of this man unsettle her so much? A week ago she'd never met him.

Why was the concept of family suddenly everywhere?

'I'll see you back at the house,' she mumbled and Hugo took her arm and led her to the door.

'I'll take you.'

'It's two minutes' walk.'

'I'll take you,' he said more firmly, and then he turned back to Terry's family. 'I'll be back in a few minutes. Joe's looking after Terry. He'll let me know the minute he's awake enough for you to see him. But, Maree, that chopper lands in an hour so it might be better to grab some clothes now...'

'We'll all be in Sydney by midday tomorrow,' her mum said. 'We can bring everything she needs.'

'And I don't need toffee apples, Mum,' Maree managed

and everyone laughed and Hugo's arm tightened around Polly's shoulders and he led her to the door.

'I do need to take Polly home,' he said. 'She's still suffering after-effects...'

'From the snake bite.' Terry's dad finished the sentence for him and came forward and took her hand—her bad hand—and gripped it and didn't even notice her wince. 'You're amazing. Thank God you came to the Valley, girl. If you'd like to stay for ever, you'd be very, very welcome.'

Her hand hurt. The grip had been hard.

Her ankle hurt.

Actually, all of her hurt. The aches and bruises that had been put on the backburner by adrenaline now started to make themselves known.

She really was wobbly. She really did need Hugo's arm around her as they headed across the path from hospital to house.

Or she told herself that. Because somehow it felt...okay.

It felt as if his hold was somehow linking her to...reality?

That was a nonsense thought, but then her head was producing a lot of nonsense at the moment.

It was his skill, she told herself. His surgeon's fingers had been amazing to watch. Skill was always a turn-on.

Skill had nothing to do with it.

Hugo was a turn-on.

She was so aware of him. She was behaving like a teenager with a crush, she decided, but the thought was fleeting because the sensation of being held, being cared for, was so infinitely sweet...

They reached the veranda steps. He took her arm and she let herself lean on him as she climbed.

She hated being cared for. Didn't she?

'I need to go back,' he said, and she heard a reluctance in his voice that matched hers. 'I need to organise transport.'

'Of course you do.'

'Polly…'

'Mmm?'

'Thank you.'

'There's no need to thank me,' she said, whispering suddenly although there was no need to whisper because there was no one to hear but Hamster, who'd wagged his tail once when they'd reached the top of the steps and then gone back to sleep. He was a dog obviously used to the comings and goings of his master. 'I believe I'm being paid.'

'Not enough,' he said and she turned and smiled. She knew her smile was shaky. She knew she was too close and she knew what she was doing was unwise—but she was doing it anyway.

'I'd do it for free,' she murmured and his smile suddenly faded and so did hers. And his hands came out to take hers and almost unconsciously—as if she had no say in what was happening at all—she tilted her chin in a gesture that meant only one thing.

That meant he had nothing to do but lower his mouth to hers.

That meant he had nothing to do but kiss her.

She'd never been kissed like this.

She must have been, she thought dazedly. She'd had boyfriends since her early teens. Her mum had been matchmaking for ever, and Polly wasn't exactly a shrinking violet. Boyfriends were fun. Kissing was nice.

This kissing wasn't nice. This kiss was…

Mind-blowing. There were no other words big enough, for from the moment his mouth met hers she seemed to be melting. It was as if his body was somehow merging into hers, supporting her, warming her, becoming part of her.

Her senses were exploding.

His mouth enveloped hers and all she could do was taste him, feel him, want him. She was kissing with a fierceness that almost frightened her.

She'd never been out of control with her boyfriends. She dated 'nice' boys.

This was no nice boy. This was a man who was as hungry as she was, as demanding, as committed...

Hungry? Demanding? Committed? That described her. She could be none of those things, yet right now she was all three. She surrendered herself to his kiss and she gloried in it. Her fingers entwined themselves in his hair, tugging him closer. She was standing on tiptoe but his arms were around her waist, pulling her up, so the kiss could sink deeper...

She was on fire.

Hugo... His name was a whisper, a shout, a declaration all by itself. Pollyanna Hargreaves was right out of her comfort zone. She was right out of control.

If he picked her up and carried her to his bed right now, would she submit?

There was no *submit* about it. If she had her way it'd be Polly who'd be doing the carrying. She wanted him!

She couldn't have him. Even as the crazy idea hit, the need to carry this straight through to the bedroom, he was putting her back.

It was a wrench like no other. Their mouths parted and she felt...lost.

'I need to go.' His voice was ragged. 'Terry needs...'

'Y...yes.'

He took a step back, turned away and then paused and turned back. 'That wasn't a casual kiss.'

'You could have fooled me,' she managed and he gave a twisted smile.

'Polly, what I'm feeling...'

And suddenly it was out there, this thing between them. Lust, love—whatever. Only it couldn't be love, Polly thought dazedly, because they'd only known each other for three days and no one fell in love that fast.

Lust, then. The way she was feeling...certainly it was lust.

'Yeah, I'm feeling it, too,' she managed. 'So it's just as

well you're going away soon because I'm just over a pos-
sessive boyfriend. And I don't do casual affairs, or family
either, for that matter, and you have a daughter...'

'A niece.'

'A niece.' She closed her eyes as she corrected herself.
A waif-like kid who Hugo loved. Why did that make him
seem more sexy, not less?

Why was Ruby suddenly in the equation?

'Hugo, I don't do family,' she said again and surprisingly
her voice sounded almost calm. 'That's why I'm here—to
get away from ties.'

'This isn't some kind of trap.' He said it fast.

Trap? How could she ever think of a kiss as a trap?

'Of course it's not,' she agreed. 'It was a kiss, simply that.
Excellent surgical skills always turn me on, Dr Denver.'

'So if I had warts on my nose, a sagging middle and a dis-
inclination to wash, but I removed an appendix with style,
you'd still turn into a puddle of molten passion?'

He was smiling, making things light, and she had to too.
'You'd better believe it.'

'So, on a scale of one to ten...speedy repair of ingrown
toenail?'

'Ooh, don't talk dirty,' she managed and scraped up a
grin. 'Next you'll be talking laparoscopic gallstone removal
and I have no defences.'

He chuckled but it sounded forced. He was as shaken as
she was, she thought.

But they were apart now. Work was waiting and they
both knew it.

'Bed,' he said and she blinked.

'Is that an order?'

'I guess it is.'

'You're not my doctor.' It suddenly seemed important—
incredibly important—to make that clear.

'I know.' He hesitated. 'And in two weeks I won't be your
colleague.'

'And I'll be on the other side of the world.'

'Really? Where?'

'Sudan, maybe. Ethiopia.'

'With Type One Diabetes?' He sounded incredulous.

'I can cope.'

'Polly...'

'Don't fuss.'

'I'm not fussing.' Except he was, she thought, and she also thought, with a modicum of self-knowledge, that she'd driven him to fuss. It was like someone with one leg declaring they intended to be a tightrope walker.

She could probably do it.

Her parents would worry.

This man might too, and by making such a declaration... it had been like a slap. *Fuss if you dare; it'll give me an excuse to run.*

It wasn't fair.

'Go,' she told him. 'Work's waiting. The chopper should be here soon.'

'Yes.' But still there was hesitation.

'The kiss was a mistake,' she said. 'An aberration.'

'We both know it was no such thing, but I can't push. I have no right. Polly...'

'Go,' she said. 'No such thing or not, I'm completely uninterested.'

Hugo headed back to the hospital feeling...empty. Gutted?

What had just happened?

He'd been knocked back. He'd kissed her. She'd responded with passion but that passion had given way to sense. She was fiercely independent and wanted to be more so. He had a commitment that would tie him here for life.

He was trapped here. How could he possibly ask a woman to share this trap?

Maybe he could move back to Sydney. Maybe he could

pick up the strings of the life he'd known before. He moved in the circles Polly moved in...

Except she wasn't going back to Sydney. She was escaping family and he had Ruby. The life he had in Sydney was over.

The thought of Sydney was like a siren song. He could go back to performing the surgery he'd trained for. He was picking up his family medicine skills here, but the surgical skills he'd fought to gain...to let them fade...

He had no choice but to let them go. Ruby had lost far more than he had. He could take Ruby back to Sydney— of course he could—but apartment life wouldn't suit her or Hamster. He'd be back working twelve-hour days. Ruby wouldn't be surrounded by people who cared about her.

His trap had firmly closed.

He sighed and squared his shoulders and headed up the ramp to the hospital entrance.

A wallaby was sitting by the door.

'Popped in for a check-up?' he asked the little creature. The wallaby seemed to be admiring her reflection in the glass door. 'Or is there anything more urgent I can help you with?'

The wallaby turned and gazed at him, almost thoughtfully. They stared at each other for a long moment and then the helicopter appeared, low and fast, from the east. The wallaby looked up at the sky, looked again at Hugo and then bounded off, back down the ramp and into the bush.

Back to freedom. No ties there.

'I'm not jealous,' Hugo muttered as he headed through the doors and made his way to the waiting Terry. 'I can make a life here.'

Without Polly?

'And that's a stupid thought,' he told himself. 'You made that decision well before Polly came on the scene. How one red-headed, flibbertigibbet doctor can mess with your equanimity...'

'A flibbertigibbet?' he demanded of himself and he must

have said the word too loud because Joe was waiting for him
and he raised his brows in enquiry.

'The wallaby,' he explained. 'She was looking at her reflection in the glass door. She's headed back to the bush
now. I thought she might have a medical issue, but she
was probably just checking her mascara. Flibbertigibbet.
Wallabies are like that.'

'Yes, Doctor,' Joe said cautiously. 'Mate, are you...okay?'

'Never better,' he murmured. 'One more day of work and
then I'm off for Christmas holidays. Bring it on.'

'You can't wait to get out of here?'

'How can you doubt it?' he demanded, but he thought of
Polly standing on the veranda looking after him and he knew
that doubt was totally justified.

Polly stayed on the veranda for a very long time.

The kiss stayed with her.

She sank into one of the big cane chairs and Hamster
licked her hand and put his big boofy head on her knee. It
was almost as if he knew she needed comfort.

Why did she need comfort? What possible reason was
there to feel bereft?

Just because someone had kissed her...

Just because someone was impossible.

She should leave now. That was what part of her felt like
doing—packing her little sports car and driving away, fast.

That was fear talking—and why was she fearful?

Where was the new brave Polly now? The intrepid Polly
who'd walked away from her family, who'd vowed to be independent, who'd hankered after a life free of the obliga-
tions of loving?

It had all seemed so simple back in Sydney. Toss in her
hospital job. Declare her independence to her parents. Start
treating herself as a grown-up.

She wasn't feeling grown-up now. She was feeling...just
a little bit stupid.

'Which is stupid all by itself,' she told Hamster. 'Here I am, less than a week into my new life, and I'm questioning everything. I haven't given it a chance. And if I left here... where would I run to? Back to my parents? Not in a month of Sundays. Off to Ethiopia? We both know that's not going to happen. No, all I need to do is stay here, keep my feet firmly on the ground, keep lust solidly damped and get on with my work. And I'll work better if I sleep now.'

But the kiss was still with her, all around her, enveloping her in its sweetness.

'Hugo's back at work and he's probably forgotten all about it,' she told Hamster. 'Men are like that.'

Hamster whined and put a paw on her lap.

'With one exception,' she told him generously. 'And by the way, if Hugo thinks he's taking you back to that boarding place while he's away, he has another think coming. You're staying with me for Christmas.'

Because she didn't want to be alone?

The question was suddenly out there, insidious, even threatening.

She did want to be alone, she told herself. That was what this whole locum bit was about. She'd been cloistered since birth. She needed to find herself.

She didn't need Hugo.

'And he doesn't need me,' she told herself, rising and heading indoors, not because she wanted to but because it was sensible and a woman had to be sensible. She had the remnants of a snake bite and a cut hand to take care of. Medicine... That was what she was here for, and that was what she needed to focus on.

'And nothing else,' she told herself as she passed the tree in the living room with Ruby's stack of origami gifts.

She hoped Ruby was having a happy sleepover with her friend tonight.

'But that's nothing to do with me either,' she told Hamster and she took a couple of deep breaths and poured herself a glass of juice for her bedside, because a woman had to be sensible.

'That's the new me,' she told Hamster as she headed for her bedroom. 'Sensible R Us. I'm Dr Pollyanna Hargreaves, with the frivolous name, but there's nothing else frivolous about me. I'm here to focus on medicine and nothing else. I will not think about Hugo Denver. Not one bit.'

She lied.

She went to bed and lay in the dark and all she could think of was Hugo. All she could feel was Hugo. His kiss enveloped her dreams and she tossed and turned and decided that snake bite venom was insidious.

It had turned one sensible doctor into an idiot.

CHAPTER ELEVEN

POLLY WOKE AND rain was thundering on the roof. It wasn't a shower. This was a deluge.

In Sydney—in fact in any house or hotel she'd ever stayed in—she hardly heard the rain. At most it was a hushed background whisper. Here it was crashing so hard on the iron roof she figured she could sing Christmas carols out loud and no one would hear.

Why not? She did.

Ruby heard her. Two bars into 'Silent Night' there was a scratching on the door. She called, 'Come in,' and Ruby flew in to land on the bed beside her. Hamster arrived straight after. He was wet. Very wet. He leaped onto her bedcovers and shook and Polly yelped and Ruby gave a tentative giggle. A very tentative giggle.

'Is he...is he okay?' she stammered.

Polly surveyed the dog with disgust. He appeared to have taken a mud bath or six.

'He appears okay. Is there a problem?'

'He's scared of thunder. He was outside jumping in puddles when the last bit of thunder came. We got scared.'

'Where's your uncle?' Hamster's wetness was soaking her feet. So much for a nice invalidish sleep-in, she thought, and resigned herself.

'He's over at the hospital.'

'Why are you home?'

'There was thunder in the night. I got scared too, so Talia's mum rang Uncle Hugo and he came and got me.'

So even if they'd indulged in a night of molten passion

they would have been hit by kid-interruptus, Polly thought, and then snagged her errant thoughts and shoved them in the place in her brain marked 'Inappropriate'.

'It's raining a lot,' Ruby said, snuggling into Polly's bed as if she had every right to be there. 'Uncle Hugo says it's raining even in Sydney but it'll stop by Christmas so that's okay. And we're leaving first thing in the morning as long as you're better. But he says you're almost better anyway. He says I can stay here with you this morning. He says you have to stay in bed until at least ten o'clock. He says Hamster and I can make you toast but we can't make you coffee because I'm not allowed to use the kettle yet.'

'Your Uncle Hugo is bossy.'

'Yes,' Ruby said happily. 'I like it. My mum wasn't bossy. One day I had to make her a cup of tea and I burned myself. See my scar?' She held up a wrist, where a scar showed the burn had been small but significant. 'Uncle Hugo said Mum shouldn't have asked me but he said she only did 'cos she was sick. But he's not sick so he's allowed to be bossy.'

'And he's at the hospital?'

'Mr Millard's cow got bogged.' Ruby was right under the covers now, nudging Hamster's rear end with her feet. The dog was heaving up and down but grinning his dopey Labrador smile, thunder forgotten. 'And Mr Millard pulled it out with a rope but he fell over when it came out fast. He broke his arm and Uncle Hugo has to put plaster on it. But Polly, I've been looking at our presents and worrying. We won't have a Christmas tree at the beach. Uncle Hugo says it doesn't matter but I think we need one.'

'You definitely need one. You can take mine,' Polly offered.

'But what will you and Hamster have?'

'We'll chop down a gum tree.'

'With an axe?'

'Yes.'

'Uncle Hugo won't let you use an axe.'

'Uncle Hugo's not the boss of me.'

'He just doesn't want us to get burned,' Ruby said worriedly. 'You might hurt yourself.

'I can take care of myself. I'm a grown-up.'

'My mum was a grown-up and she didn't take care of herself. She died.'

There was no answer to that. Another clap of thunder rumbled across the valley. Hamster turned into a quivering mess; Polly and Ruby had to hug him and then the whole bed was pretty much a quivering and soggy mess and Polly decided convalescence had knobs on and she might as well get up.

'You would like to take my Christmas tree?'

Ruby looked through to the living room where the sparkling silver tree shimmered with its party lights on full. 'I don't want you not to have one,' she said longingly, 'but you aren't allowed to use the axe.'

'I'll let Uncle Hugo wield the axe,' Polly conceded. 'But we need more decorations. You're not going to leave me with nothing.'

'We could buy more tinsel.'

'Nonsense.' She was in her element here. Interior decorating had been bred into her—her mother had been making hotel rooms into Christmas-themed fantasies for ever. 'Let's leave the silver tree as it is—we'll pack it tonight for you to take. Then we'll concentrate on Tree Two. Plus making this house Christmassy for me and Hamster. Let's go.'

By two in the afternoon the inhabitants of Wombat Valley were mostly hunkered down. The weather forecast was dire. Leaving the house meant a soaking. Most minor ailments could be put in the worry-about-it-after-Christmas basket, so the population mostly stayed put.

Which meant Hugo didn't call on Polly for help.

Though maybe he should have, he thought as the day went on. The agreement was that she'd join him in the afternoon so she'd get used to the place and he could assess her work…

Except he had assessed her work and it was excellent. She'd given last night's anaesthetic with skill. On her tour of the place she'd moved seamlessly between patients, chatting happily, drawing them out without them realising it. Underneath the chat there were carefully planted medical queries, and skilled responses to the replies. She was good.

More, Polly's reputation had already spread through the Valley. She was the Doc-Who'd-Been-Bitten-Saving-Horace. Horace wasn't particularly popular but he was a local, and Wombat Valley looked after their own.

So she was already accepted. She already knew her way round the hospital. She could have another full day of rest.

Minding Ruby?

He did feel a bit guilty about that, but he'd assumed Ruby would stay at Talia's until midday so he hadn't worried about calling anyone in. And Ruby was quiet. She did her own thing. The monitor was on. He could be home in a heartbeat if he was needed.

He just sort of happened to wander past the monitor a lot.

'They sound like they're having a ball,' Joe told him. Joe was catching up on paperwork at the nurses' station. The whole hospital seemed as if it was snoozing, and in the silence Polly and Ruby's voices could be heard clearly.

He'd told Polly about the monitor. She'd know whatever she was saying could be overheard but it didn't seem to be cramping her style.

'The flour looks great. No, sprinkle some more on, Ruby, it looks like snow. Hamster, no! It's snow, you idiot, not flour. Oh, heck, it's on your nose—no, don't lick it, it'll turn to paste—no, Hamster, noooo...'

'Uh oh,' Joe said, grinning. 'When my kids sound like that I go in armed with a mop. You want to go home and check?'

'I should...'

'Should what?' Joe said, and eyed him speculatively. 'Think of something else to do? You've been thinking of other something elses to do for the past two hours. Don't you need to pack?'

'I've packed.'

'Then don't you need to go home and spread a little flour?' His brows went up. 'But Dr Hargreaves is there, isn't she? A woman in your living room.'

'With my niece,' he snapped.

'She's gorgeous,' Joe said.

'Ruby's cute.'

'I didn't mean Ruby and you know it. Polly's gorgeous. We're lucky to have her.'

'Yes.'

'But you're going away tomorrow.' His nurse administrator's eyebrows were still raised. 'Not having any second thoughts about going?'

'Only in as much as Polly needs care.'

'Care?'

'She's diabetic.'

'And I have a bung knee. We can commiserate.' Still the speculative look. 'So why don't you want to go home now?'

Because I might want to kiss her again.

Because I do want to kiss her.

Neither of those thoughts he could say aloud. Neither of those thoughts he should even admit to himself.

Polly…a wealthy socialite, a woman who was here for two weeks while he was away, a woman who…

Made Ruby chuckle.

A woman who made him want to pick her up and carry her to his bed.

A woman who he wouldn't mind protecting for the rest of her life.

Whoa… How to go on a hundred-mile journey in four days. He didn't know her. She was so far out of his league…

But he was there. He wanted her.

'Go home,' Joe said, watching his face, and Hugo wondered how much of what he'd been thinking was plain to see. 'Go and spend some time with her. Heaven knows, you could use a friend.'

'I have friends.'

'None like Polly,' Joe retorted. 'And isn't that just the problem? I'd go nuts without my Hannah, but for you... My Hannah's already taken and there's a limited dating field in the Valley. And now you have Pollyanna right in your living room.' He paused as Polly's infectious chuckle sounded through the monitor. 'Hannah or not, wow, Doc, I'm almost tempted to head over there myself.'

'I'll go when it stops raining.'

'Like that'll happen,' Joe said morosely. 'Forty days and forty nights... This is setting in bad. But it's not raining women, not on your parade...'

'Joe...'

'I know; it's none of my business.' Joe held up his hands as if in surrender. 'But she's there, she's gorgeous and you have no reason not to be there too. Go on, get out of here. Go.'

He went. Of course he went—there was no reason not to.

It was wet and it was windy. He opened the front door and was met by a squeal of protest.

'Uncle Hugo, noooooooo!'

'Uh oh,' said another voice and he stared around in amazement. The other voice said, 'Maybe you could shut the door?'

The door opened straight into the living room. The living room was...white.

Very white.

'We may not have thought this through,' Polly said.

She was sitting on the floor threading popcorn onto string. Or she had been threading popcorn. She was now coated in a cloud of flour. It was all over her hair, over her face and nose, over the floor around her.

Over Hamster.

Ruby was closest to the door. She seemed to have escaped the worst of the dusting.

'You made it blow,' she said accusingly as he finally closed out the gale.

'Flour?' he said, and his niece sent him a look that put him right in the dunce's corner.

'It's snow. We made a nativity scene. See, we've made everything out of pods from the banksia tree, even the camels, and we got really wet looking for the right banksias, and then we spent ages getting everything dry so we could put them up along the mantelpiece and we put flour over the bottom to look like snow only Polly said I probably put too much on, but it looked *beeeyootiful* but now you've opened the door and you've ruined it.'

And her voice wobbled.

She really was fragile, Hugo thought, bending down to give her a hug. Last year had been tragedy for Ruby, and it still showed. She expected calamity.

'This isn't ruined,' he said gently. 'It's just flour.'

'It's snow to make Polly feel better when we're not here.'

'And Polly loves it,' Polly said and then she sneezed as if she needed to accentuate the point. 'Ruby, it's still great. Look what we've done, Dr Denver. All we need you to do is chop down a tree.'

'With an axe,' Ruby added. 'I wouldn't let Polly do it on her own.'

'Very wise,' Hugo said faintly, looking round his living room again.

At chaos.

His mother had kept this room perfect. 'The Queen could walk in unannounced and I'd be ready for her,' his mother used to say and she was right. His mother might even have made Her Majesty remove her shoes and leave the corgis outside.

'It was wet,' Ruby said, noticing his sweep of the room

and getting in first with her excuse. 'Polly needed something to do.'

'And now she has something else to do,' Polly decreed, using Hamster as a lever to push herself to her feet. 'In case you haven't noticed, Dr Denver, you seem to be dripping on our snow and our type of snow, when dripped upon, makes clag. So I suggest you stop dripping and start helping thread popcorn while I clean up your mess...'

'My mess?'

'Your mess,' she said and grinned. 'Walking in on artists at work...you should know better.'

'I'm glad I didn't,' he said faintly and he looked around at the mess and he thought for the first time in how long... this place looked like home.

What was better than this? he thought.

What was better than Polly?

He chopped down a Christmas...branch?...while the girls admired his axe technique. They all got wet, but what the heck; he was beyond caring. The branch dripped as he carried it inside but there was so much mess anyway that a little more wouldn't hurt. Then he cooked while they decorated.

He cooked spaghetti and meatballs because that was his speciality. Actually, he had three. Macaroni cheese was another. He could also do a mean risotto but Ruby didn't like it, so to say their menu was limited would be an understatement. But Ruby munched through raw veggies and fruit to stop him feeling guilty and Polly sat down in front of her meatballs and said, 'Yum,' as if she meant it.

They now had two Christmas trees. Ruby had declared Polly's silver tree was too pretty to take down until the last minute so there was a tree in each corner of the living room. There was 'snow' on every flat surface. There were strings of popcorn and paper chains and lanterns and Polly's amazing gift boxes, plus the weird decorations and nativity figures they'd fashioned out of banksia pods.

Polly ate her dinner but every now and then he caught her looking through to the sitting room and beaming.

She'd dressed for dinner. She was wearing another of her retro dresses. This one had splashes of crimson, yellow and blue, and was cinched at the waist with a shiny red belt. The dress had puffed sleeves and a white collar and cuff trim.

Her curls were shining. Her freckles were…freckling. She did not look like a doctor.

She looked adorable.

He didn't want to leave tomorrow.

How could he fall for a woman called Pollyanna?

How could he not?

'We've done good,' Polly was saying to Ruby and Ruby looked where Polly was looking and nodded her agreement.

'Yes. But you'll be here by yourself.' She sounded worried.

'Me and Hamster,' Polly reminded her. 'I'm glad your uncle agreed to let him stay. I might be lonely without him.'

'Won't you be lonely without your mum and dad?' Ruby asked and Polly's smile died.

'No.'

'Won't they be lonely without you?'

There was an uncomfortable silence. Polly ate another meatball but she suddenly didn't seem so hungry.

'They have lots of friends,' she said at last. 'They've booked a restaurant. They'll have a very good party.'

'It won't be much fun if you're not there.'

'They'll hardly miss me,' Polly said stoutly. 'Whereas if I wasn't here Hamster would miss me a lot. Plus Hazel Blacksmith's promised to teach me to tat.'

'Tat,' Hugo said faintly. 'What on earth is tat?'

'You come back after Christmas and I'll show you. Whatever it is, the house will be full of it.'

'That'll make a nice change from soggy flour.'

'Bah! Humbug!' she said cheerfully and got up to clear the dishes. Instead of getting up to help, he let himself sit for a moment, watching her, watching Ruby jump up to help, feeling himself...wanting.

It wasn't fair to want. He had no right.

To try and saddle her with Wombat Valley and a needy seven-year-old? And...

And what was he thinking?

He was trapped. He had no right to think of sharing.

At Ruby's request, Polly read her a bedtime story while Hugo did a last fast ward round. The hospital was quiet. The rain had stopped, the storm was over and what was left was peace. The night before Christmas? Not quite, but it might just as well be, he thought. The whole Valley seemed to be settling, waiting...

Waiting? There was nothing to wait for.

Of course there was, he told himself as he headed back to the house. He was heading to the beach tomorrow. Ten glorious days of freedom.

With Ruby.

He wouldn't have it any other way, he told himself, but he knew a part of him was lying. His sister's suicide had killed the part that enjoyed being a skilled surgeon in a tight-knit surgical team. It had killed the guy who could head to the bar after work and stay as late as he wanted. It had killed the guy who could date who he wanted...

And it was the last thing that was bugging him now.

Dating who he wanted...

Polly.

He wanted Polly.

And she was waiting for him. The light was fading. She was sitting on the old cane chair on the veranda, Hamster at her side. She smiled as he came up the steps and he had such a powerful sense of coming home...

He wanted to walk straight to her, gather her into his arms and claim her as his own. It was a primitive urge, totally inappropriate, totally without consideration, but the urge was so strong he held onto the veranda rail, just to ground himself.

Do not do anything stupid, he told himself. *This woman's ethereal, like a butterfly. You'll be gone tomorrow and when you return she'll flit on. Life will close in on you again. Accept it.*

'Ruby's asleep,' Polly said, leaning back in the rocker and rocking with satisfaction. 'I read her to sleep. Boring R Us.'

Nothing about this woman was boring, he thought, but he managed to make his voice almost normal. 'What did you read?'

'*The Night Before Christmas*, of course,' she told him. 'I just happen to have a copy in my luggage.'

'Of course you do.'

'My nannies read it to me every Christmas.' She sailed on serenely, oblivious to his dry interruption. 'I started asking for it to be read about mid-November every year. I can't believe you don't own it.'

'My mother didn't believe in fairy tales.'

And her eyes widened. 'Fairy tales? What's fairy tale about *The Night Before Christmas*? Next you'll be saying you don't believe in Santa.'

And Hugo thought back to the Christmases since his father died—the struggle to stay cheerful, Grace's depression—and he thought… *All we needed was a Pollyanna. A fairy tale…*

His parents had been down-to-earth, sensible people. He thought of his sister, crippled by depression. He thought of his father, terse, impatient, telling the teenage Grace to snap out of it.

Grace might still be alive, he thought suddenly, if she'd been permitted a fairy tale.

And… Life might be good for him if he could admit a fairy tale?

A fairy tale called Pollyanna?

'Polly…'

'I need your help,' she told him. 'You're leaving at crack of dawn and we need to pack the silver Christmas tree without making the living room look bereft. I don't intend to have a bereft Christmas, thank you very much.' She rocked her way forward out of the rocker and it was all he could do not to step forward and...

Not!

Somehow he managed to calmly follow her into the house and start the demolition process, following instructions as to which decorations would stay and which would go.

'I wonder if I could make a tatted angel for your tree next year,' she mused as she packed golden balls into a crimson box. It seemed even the crates she stored things in were a celebration. 'What do you reckon? If you get an angel in the post, will you know what to do with it? Will you value it as you ought?'

She was kneeling by the tree. The Christmas tree lights were still on, flickering multi-coloured patterns on her face. Her eyes were twinkling and a man wouldn't be human...

He didn't go to her. There was a mound of tinsel and a box of Christmas decorations between them. It had to act like Hadrian's Wall.

To stop himself scaring this butterfly into flight.

'Polly, I'd like to keep in touch,' he ventured and she went right on packing decorations as if what he'd said wasn't important.

'I'd like that too,' she said. 'But you're behind the times. Ruby and I already have it planned. We're going to be pen pals—real pen pals with letters with stamps because that's cooler than emails. Ruby will send pictures of herself, and of Hamster too, because I'm starting to think I'll miss him.'

Pen pals.

'That's good, as far as it goes,' he said cautiously. 'But it's not what I had in mind.'

'What did you have in mind?'

'The kiss,' he said and her head jerked up and the atmosphere in the room changed, just like that.

'The kiss...'

Stop now, the sensible part of him demanded, but there was a crazy part that kept putting words out there. 'It meant something,' he said. 'Polly, I'd like to keep seeing you.'

'That might be hard if you're in Wombat Valley and I'm in Ethiopia.'

'You're really thinking of Ethiopia?'

'No,' she said reluctantly. 'I can't.'

'Then how about an extension of your time in Wombat Valley?'

The question hung. It had been dumb to even ask, he thought, but he couldn't retract the words now.

'Stay here, you mean?' she said cautiously.

'We could...just see.'

'See what?' Her eyes didn't leave his face.

'If you and I...'

'I don't do family.' She stumbled to her feet and a crimson ball fell onto another and shattered. She didn't appear to notice.

'Polly, this isn't a proposal.' What had he done? He was appalled at the look of fear that had flashed across her face. 'I'm not asking for permanent. It's far too soon...'

'It's not only too soon,' she snapped. 'It's stupid.'

'Why is it stupid?' He knew, but he still found himself asking. Did she know what a trap his life was?

But it seemed she was worrying about a different kind of trap. 'Hugo, it's true, I kissed you and I felt...like I might be falling for you,' she managed. 'But it scared me. I don't want to go there. I can't. You worry about me, and Ruby hugs me, and even Hamster wriggles his way round my heart like a great hairy worm. But I came here to get away from family, not to find myself more.'

Her words cut, but they were no more than he'd expected.

To hope for more was stupid.

So now what? There was a strained silence while he tried to find a way forward. He'd thought he'd put away his love life when he'd left Sydney, but somehow Polly had hauled it front and centre. He wanted...a woman like Polly?

No. He wanted Polly herself, yet he had no right to haul her into his own personal drama. How could he possibly think of adding his constraints to hers? There was no way through this tangle to a happy ending.

So now? Now he had to get this situation back to a relationship that could go forward as it should. Employer and employee, nothing more.

'You don't think you might be propelling things forward just a tad too fast?' he ventured. 'I'm not asking you to commit to Wombat Valley for life.' He tried smiling, aching to ease her look of fear, but the fear stayed. It seemed she wasn't good at pretending. The employer, employee relationship was finished.

'Hugo, I know what I felt—when I kissed you.' She put her hands behind her and took a step back. 'When I'm with you I feel like someone else. It would be so easy to fall into this place, become your lover, become Ruby's best friend, become Hamster's third favourite cushion, but you'd tie me down. You'd fret—you already do—and before I know it you'd be watching what I eat and checking my long-term sugar levels and making sure I wear warm coats and boots when it's raining and not letting me do the hard medical cases because it might upset me. And I'm sick of cotton wool; I'm just...over it.'

'Polly, of all the things I'm offering, cotton wool isn't one of them.'

'You're saying you wouldn't fuss?'

'Warm coats, boots, the Hamster cushion thing...all those things are negotiable,' he said evenly. 'But if we ever tried it...maybe you couldn't stop me caring.' He had to be honest. 'I'd hope you could care back.'

'I don't do caring.'

'I've watched you for days now. You care and you care and you care.'

'Not with you.'

There was nothing to say to that. Nothing at all.

He'd been stupid to ask. This place—his life—had nothing a woman like Polly would wish to share. How could he ever have imagined otherwise?

He looked at her for a long moment and then, because he couldn't think of anything else to do, he started untangling tinsel. And Polly knelt again to put decorations into boxes.

'There's broken glass by your knee. Be careful.'

'I know,' she snapped, but she hadn't noticed—he knew she hadn't. She looked and saw the shattered Christmas bauble. 'Thank...thank you.'

'I'll get the dustpan.'

'I broke it. I'll fix it.'

'Fine,' he said and then his cellphone rang and he was almost relieved. He went outside to answer it because he needed space.

He felt like smacking himself over the head. For one brief moment he'd tried to prise open the doors that enclosed him. All he'd done was frighten her.

Where to take it from here?

Nowhere.

She was an idiot.

She gathered the shards of glass and then got the vacuum cleaner because you could never be too careful with glass on carpet and she wasn't stupid...

She was stupid, stupid, stupid.

For heaven's sake... He wasn't asking her to marry him, she told herself. He was simply asking her to extend her time here as a locum.

Ruby would love it. Hamster would love it.

Polly would love it?

Love... The word echoed round and round in her head. She hit the power switch to the vacuum cleaner so it faded to silence and she gazed round at the mess that was the living room.

Mess. Christmas.

Family.

She didn't do family. She hated Christmas.

But still she was staring around the room. One intact Christmas branch, gaily decorated. One lopsided silver tree, semi naked. Hugo saw this place as a trap, she thought. A prison. Oh, but if she let herself care...

If she cared, he'd care right back, and the cotton wool would enclose her.

'It's a mess,' she muttered to herself and suddenly she found herself thinking of her parents' Christmases. They were perfection in planning and execution. Exquisite. Her mother employed party planners.

There'd be no soggy flour on her mother's carpet. The only thing missing from her family's perfect Christmas this year would be her.

And, stupidly, she felt tears well behind her eyes. She dashed them away with an angry swipe. *What the heck...* She didn't cry. She never cried.

She'd walked away from her family Christmas without a second glance. She'd felt joyful to be escaping.

And here was Hugo offering her another family Christmas. Not yet, she thought, not this Christmas, but she knew his offer was like an insidious web—*'Come into my parlour,' said the spider to the fly...*

Only it wasn't like that. What fly had ever thought the spider doing the inviting was gorgeous? What spider was ever kind, skilled, gentle, loving, awesome...?

Stop it, stop it, stop it, she told her spinning head. *You've refused him and there's an end to it. You don't want to be caged. Get your head in order and get on with cleaning up this mess.*

And then Hugo walked back into the room and one look at his face told her cleaning had to be put onto the backburner.

CHAPTER TWELVE

'TROUBLE?' POLLY DIDN'T have to ask but she did anyway. Vacuum cleaning was forgotten.

'I need to go out.'

'Tell me.'

'If you could look after Ruby…'

'Tell me,' she snapped again and he paused at the door and looked at her—really looked—and she could almost see the struggle to transform her from a ditzy woman in a rainbow dress to someone who might just be a colleague.

She dropped the vacuum cleaner to help the transition. She thought about white coats but there was hardly time.

'There's been a landslide,' he said.

A landslide…

The rain had stopped now, but it had been torrential. With the steepness of this valley, landslides had to be an ever-present danger.

'I need to go…'

'Tell me,' she said for a third time and he got it then. She wasn't a ditzy redhead. She was an Emergency Medicine specialist and she was demanding facts.

And he switched, just like that. As unlikely a setting as this was, in that moment they joined forces.

A medical team.

'On the road to the south,' he told her. 'We already have trouble. The north road's still cut where Horace's truck went over. Everyone's been using the south road. But Ben Smart's cow got out and wandered down the road this morning in the rain. A petrol tanker came through and wiped the cow.

That wasn't a problem—apart from the cow. The tanker had bull bars. But Ben's cow was left dead on the side of the road and Iris and Gladys Freeman live right where it was hit and they don't want a dead cow smelling up their Christmas.'

He headed for his bedroom as he spoke, hauling on his jacket, speaking to her through the open door.

'Ben's not all that addicted to hard work,' he threw at her. 'But Iris and Gladys were insistent, so Ben got his brother and they looked at the dead cow and thought how hard it would be to bury her. They're Smart by name but not by nature. They looked at the nice soggy side of the cliff face and thought they could just dig a bit and shove her in.'

'Uh oh.' Polly was heading into her bedroom too. Jeans, she thought. Jacket. And shoes. Sensible shoes would be important.

Did snakes come out after rain?

'So...' she called out from the bedroom. 'Situation?'

'The whole side of the hill's come down. Ben's brother, Doug, seems to have a broken leg but he got himself out. Ben was completely buried for a bit. Amy and Max Fraser were there first—they're sensible farmers. Amy's an ex-nurse. She says Ben's in a bad way. Oh, and Iris and Gladys are there too, but Iris has fallen over and Gladys has hurt her back. I might be a while.' And then she emerged from her bedroom and he was in the living room and he looked at her jeans and jacket and boots. 'What the...?'

'I'm coming too. Incident with multiple casualties. Why question it?'

'Ruby?'

'Excuse me? Am I here as a childminder?'

'No, but...'

'Isn't Ruby asleep?'

'Yes...'

'And isn't your normal child care system working?'

'Polly, you can't. You're three days post-snake-bite.'

'Yeah and you'll be post-kick-on-the-shins if you fuss for

no reason,' she snapped. 'Do what you must to let the hospital know Ruby needs monitoring. Then let's go.'

What confronted them could have been a tragedy. It was bad, but by the time they got there Ben was sitting up, retching mud and wheezing. He was still gasping but at least he was conscious.

Iris and Gladys, two very elderly ladies, were fussing over him and berating him at the same time.

'We had to do CPR for ages.' Iris, an indomitable lady who looked to be in her nineties, was sitting back on her heels, glaring as if she wanted to punch Ben again. 'I hit him so hard to get him breathing before Amy and Max arrived that I've hurt my wrists, and then he threw up on my dressing gown. And I'll never get it dry in this weather.'

All this and she was complaining about the weather? Polly and Hugo shared a grin as they set to work.

Ben was indeed all right. He'd been momentarily buried in the mud. Luckily, Amy and Max had had a shovel on their truck and had done some fast digging. Amy was now tending to Doug, who lay beside his brother, moaning in pain.

Doug's leg was fractured. His patience with his brother had snapped completely.

'That's the last time I'm gonna agree to one of his harebrained schemes. "It'll be easy," he said. "Just dig a bit into the cliff and shove her in and we won't even have to move her".'

The cow, thankfully, was now buried, but at what a cost?

'You've succeeded, you idiots,' Max said dourly. 'You've also succeeded in cutting the road. The north road's still impassable so we're stuck. The town'll have your guts for garters, guys. Just saying.'

But while he was talking, Hugo and Polly had moved into triage mode, figuring what needed to be done and doing it with the ease of a team that had worked together for years. Polly was wiping the mud from Ben's face, checking his mouth, his nose, his neck. She was preparing an oxygen mask. Ben was breathing but his colour was poor. Assuming his breathing had stopped, even for a moment, it was important to get his oxygen levels up.

Hugo was administering morphine to Doug, then slitting his pants leg to expose the leg break. Polly glanced over and saw no exposed bone, no break in the skin.

They might be lucky, she thought. Doug looked well into his seventies, maybe early eighties. Even a simple fracture would take time to heal but a compound fracture could be disastrous.

'I think you've been lucky,' Hugo told him, confirming what she was thinking. 'Okay, without moving anything—head, neck, arms or legs—let's do a bit of wiggle checking.'

She did the same for Ben, carefully checking each limb. She fitted a neck brace as a precaution—if the dirt had come down on his head she wanted an X-ray before she let him move.

'We'll need to get everyone to hospital,' Hugo told her. 'I want a proper examination.' He turned to Gladys who looked, if anything, even older and more withered than her sister. 'Max said you hurt your back.'

'It's a twinge,' Gladys said with dignity. 'We had to pull to try and get this idiot's head out. Iris fell over—look at her first.'

Iris had indeed fallen over. She had a long graze, the length of her shin.

There was another exchanged glance between Hugo and Polly. Iris's skin was old-age-dry, scarred from years of bumps and bruises and varicose veins. It'd be a miracle if her leg didn't ulcerate. And Gladys's hands were surreptitiously going to the small of her back. Pain was obvious and both she and Hugo could see it.

'Right,' Hugo said. 'Let's get you all into the hospital where we can look at you properly. We need to do it carefully. Amy, Max, are you happy to help? Great. Can you take Iris and Gladys—they're both good to go sitting up, but drive slowly. Try not to bump. Ben and Doug, though, need to be transported flat. I have matting in the back of my van. Polly, can we do a three-way shift? Max, can you help?'

'But we're not going to the hospital,' Gladys said, astounded, and Hugo put a hand on her shoulder and met her frightened gaze with compassion.

'Gladys, how long did Iris's leg ulcer take to heal? Let's try and prevent one forming. And Iris, you can see that Gladys has hurt her back. Do you really not want me to see what the damage is? Won't you let me see if I can stop it hurting for Christmas?'

And, put like that, heading to the hospital for each other, there was no choice.

'We need to ring a couple of local farmers.' Hugo had been carrying lanterns in his truck. So had Amy and Max, so the scene they were working in was lit, but to the north there was a sea of mud where the road should be. 'We'll need to set up road blocks and warning lamps.'

'Can't we get the ambulance?' Polly asked. 'Surely it'd be better to wait.' The ambulance had proper stretchers—a much safer way of carrying patients with potential spinal injuries. To put them in Hugo's van…

'We can't do it,' Hugo said grimly. 'We share the ambulance service with Willaura. They're fifteen miles down the road, on the far side of the land slip. Given that the south road's cut and now the north road… Sorry, guys, the truck it is.'

They worked solidly for the next few hours. Each of the four, although not dangerously injured, had their own urgent needs. Ben had swallowed—and inhaled—dirty water and mud. He needed intravenous antibiotics. Doug's leg needed setting. Luckily, it was a simple tibial break but he was a pack a day smoker. He coughed and wheezed and the decision was admission, oxygen and observation.

They admitted Gladys and Iris, too. Gladys's back showed little damage apart from osteoarthritic change but she was more shaken than she'd admit. Iris's leg needed scrupulous cleaning and dressing, and once they'd got over their first protests the elderly ladies seemed content to be fussed over.

'And you do need to let us fuss over you,' Polly declared as she tucked them in for the night. 'You're both heroes.'

'I agree.' Hugo must have finished at the same time as she did. He was suddenly standing at the ward door, smiling warmly at the two old ladies. 'Heroes, both of you. Max tells me even though you didn't have a spade, by the time he got there you'd already got Ben's head clear.'

'We're gardeners,' Iris said as if that explained everything.

'But we're tired gardeners,' Gladys whispered and snuggled down a bit further on her pillows. Polly had given them both pain relief and they seemed dozily content. 'Thank you, dear.'

And Hugo grinned and crossed to each of them and planted a kiss on each elderly cheek.

'No. Thank you. You've saved Ben's life.'

'Well, we're much happier being kissed by you than by Ben,' Gladys said and she giggled, and Hugo and Polly slipped out of the ward and left them to sleep.

Drama over. They could go home.

They walked in silence across the small distance that separated house from hospital. The silence between them was strained. Almost as soon as the hospital doors closed behind them they seemed no longer colleagues.

What then? Friends?

Ha.

But that was how they had to act, Polly thought, at least until tomorrow.

And with thought came another...

'Hugo... If the roads are cut in both directions... You won't be able to leave.'

Hugo didn't break stride. 'You think I don't know that?'

The surge of anger in his voice was almost shocking. 'That road can't be made safe until it dries out, and the engineers have already assessed the other road. They need to blast further into the cliff to make it safe.'

'So that would be…after Christmas?' She could hardly make herself say it but it had to be said. 'Ruby will break her heart.'

'She'll understand.' But the anger was still in his voice. 'I'll show her the roads.'

'And she'll be stoic,' Polly whispered. 'I don't think I can bear it.'

'So how the hell do you think it makes me feel?' His words were an explosion. He stopped and closed his eyes and she could see the pain, the fury that fate had once again messed with his plans for his little niece's Christmas. 'How am I going to tell her?'

'Oh, Hugo…'

'I meant the Valley to be her base, her one sense of continuity. Now it's like a trap.'

'A trap for you both?' she ventured and he stared at her for one long baffled moment and then dug his hands deep in his pockets and started walking again.

Polly didn't move on. She stood and watched his retreating back.

She couldn't help him. Not without…

No. She couldn't help him.

Or could she?

Her parents' money… Her parents' power and resources…

They could get a chopper here first thing tomorrow, she thought. Hugo and Ruby could be at the beach long before they could ever have driven.

But how could she ask that of her parents? She thought of the look on her parents' faces as she'd told them she wouldn't spend this Christmas with them. They'd been gutted. So now…

How could she tell them where she was, ask them for such a favour and then tell them to leave her alone?

Family... Love...

She stood stock-still in the darkness while her thoughts headed off in so many tangents she felt dizzy.

She should be home for Christmas.

She wasn't home. She was here. And so was Hugo because he'd chosen this place—because of love.

'Polly? What's wrong?' Hugo had reached the gate into the house yard and had turned back to see what was keeping her.

'Nothing,' she said in a small voice. 'Just...recalibrating. I guess this means...Christmas together.'

'Can we keep our hands off each other until the roads clear?' He tried to say it with humour but she heard the strain.

'I'll do my best.' She walked towards him in the darkness, but there was a part of her that said she should retreat.

She was as trapped as he was. But...define trap? Some traps you had to walk right into.

'Polly...' She was too close now, she thought, but she couldn't retreat. She was close enough to...close enough to ask for what she wanted?

'If you kiss me,' she managed, 'I think I might crack.'

'I've already cracked,' he said roughly, still with that edge of anger. 'Because all I want to do is kiss you.'

'And where will that leave us?'

'Together until after Christmas? Time for one mad passionate affair?' He snapped the words as if she'd been taunting him. 'Crazy.'

But what if it's not so crazy? It was her heart doing the thinking, not her head. *What if I want to stay? What if I don't think this is a trap at all?*

The thought was almost terrifying. How could she think of staying? She'd railed around the confines of her parents' loving. How much more would she hate the confines of being here?

Of being loved by Hugo?

'You're looking scared,' he said, suddenly gentle, and she wished he wouldn't say things gently because it was almost her undoing. His voice made things twist inside—things she seemed to be unable to untwist.

She wanted him.

They were between house and hospital—no man's land. Medicine and home.

She'd used her career to escape from home, Polly thought with sudden clarity. Maybe that was driving her nuts now. In her world of medicine, she could forget the confines of her parents' worry, her parents' overwhelming adoration. She could be Dr Hargreaves, known for her over-the-top dress sense but respected for her medical skills.

Here, between hospital and home, nothing seemed clear.

Hugo was standing beside her. He was her colleague, except he wasn't a colleague. He was just... Hugo.

How could a heart be so twisted?

How could he be so near and not reach for her?

And in the end, because the silence was stretching and she didn't know how to step away and it seemed that he didn't either, it was Polly who reached for Hugo.

She put her hands up to his face and she cupped his bristled jaw.

'You are the nicest man, Dr Denver...'

'Polly, I can't...'

'One kiss before bedtime,' she whispered and she raised herself on tiptoe. She tugged his head down, her lips met his and she kissed him.

She kissed him, hard and sure and true. She kissed him as she'd never kissed a man before and doubted if she could ever kiss a man again. It was a kiss of aching want. This was a kiss that came from a part of her she hadn't known existed.

But he didn't respond. His arms didn't come around her. He didn't kiss back.

He didn't push her away, but the heat she'd felt before

was now under rigid control. She could feel his tension, his strength, the power of his boundaries. She sank down to stand on firm ground again, feeling the first sharp shards of loss.

'Whatever I said…Polly, a short affair over Christmas is never going to work,' he managed. 'We both know that. Bad idea.'

'It is a bad idea,' she conceded.

'So we need to figure the ground rules now. No touching.'

'None?'

'Don't push me, Polly.'

And it was all there in his voice. He wanted her as much as she wanted him, but this man had already learned what it was to give up what he loved. How much had he hated to give up his surgical career, his friends, his lifestyle? He'd done it for love.

How could she ask him to give up more? An affair and then walk away? It'd hurt her. How much more would it hurt Hugo, who had no power to follow?

She had to be very sure…

'Okay, no touching,' she managed. 'I might…I might as well go to bed, then.'

'That's a good idea.' He touched her cheek—which was breaking the rules but maybe they didn't start until morning. He traced the line of her face with a gentleness she found unbearably erotic. But then, 'Sleep well, Polly,' he told her. 'Tomorrow's Christmas Eve, the night Santa comes. Maybe the old gentleman will bring sense to the pair of us.'

He didn't follow her inside. Instead, he stood where she'd left him, staring into the darkness.

He wanted her so badly it was a physical pain. She'd kissed him and the control it had taken not to sweep her into his arms and claim her had left him dizzy.

Hell, he wanted her.

'Yeah, and Ruby wants Christmas at the beach,' he told

himself. 'And I want my career back. We can't all have what we want—you're old enough to know that.'

He knew it but it didn't stop him wanting.

He wanted Polly.

Sleep was a long time coming, and when it did it was full of dreams she had no hope of understanding.

She woke to the dawn chorus. Stupid birds, she thought, lying in her too-big bed listening to the cacophony of parrots, kookaburras and bellbirds. She wouldn't have had to put up with this in Sydney.

Christmas Eve. Her mother would be up by now, doing the flowers—a task undertaken with care for every important occasion. Then there'd be the hair salon, nails, a massage, lunch with her friends, then a nap...

Then there'd be the final gift-wrapping, followed by drinks with more friends and dinner.

And, at every step of the way, her mother would miss her.

Polly lay in bed and listened to the birds and thought about her parents' demands. Why was she suddenly feeling guilty? Her parents smothered her with love and they were constantly disappointed. Last year she'd managed to juggle leave so she could join them in Monaco on Christmas Eve, but her mother had been gutted that Polly hadn't arrived early enough to get her nails done.

'And when did you last get your hair done?' she'd demanded. 'Polly, how can you bear it?'

She smiled then, remembering her father rolling his eyes, and then she thought of her father demanding she tell them the results of her last long-term blood sugar test and telling her he'd researched a new diabetic regime being tested by a clinic in Sweden and he'd fly her there in the new year...

She was right to get away. She knew she was.

It was just...they were her parents. And somehow, looking at Hugo and Ruby, she thought...she thought...

Maybe behaviour had boundaries but love was different? Maybe running away couldn't lessen that.

She sighed and rolled over and tried to sleep a bit more and she must have succeeded because the next thing she knew there was a scratch on her bedroom door. The door flew open and Hamster landed with a flying thud, right across her stomach.

He'd left the door open and from the living room she could hear every word Hugo was saying.

'Ruby, I'm so sorry.' She could almost see Hugo. He'd be crouched in front of his little niece, she thought. Ruby would have flown up as soon as she woke, letting Hamster inside and then bounding to find her uncle. The beach. They were supposed to be leaving right now.

'There's been another accident,' Hugo was telling her. 'Ruby, the roads out of here have been cut. The storm's caused a landslide. We're just going to have to put the silver tree up again and have a two-Christmas-tree Christmas.'

There was no sound. She could have borne it better if Ruby sobbed, Polly thought, but Ruby didn't cry.

If enough was taken away from you, you expected nothing.

Like Hugo... So much had been taken away from him.

How could he expect her to love him?

Would he want her to love him?

She'd only known him for four days. Ridiculous. How could she feel this way about a man after four days?

How could she fall in love with Ruby after four days?

She could still hear Hugo's muffled voice. Maybe he was hugging. Maybe he was holding, trying to comfort...

Beach for Christmas... It was a little thing. A minor promise. Kids got over things.

Last Christmas Ruby had lost her grandmother and then her mother.

Beach for Christmas...

She heard one sob, just the one, and somehow she knew that'd be it. This kid didn't rail against fate.

Polly did, though. She put her pillow over her head and railed.

There had to be a way.

She could still ring her father, ask him to send a chopper to get them to the beach. The idea was still there but she knew it wouldn't work, or not like she hoped. Her father would be incapable of carting away Wombat Valley's permanent doctor and leaving his daughter on her own.

What would he do? Cart her away by force? Not quite, but he wouldn't leave her here.

And with that thought came another. It was a thought so ridiculous... So over the top...

She was trying to escape her parents. She was trying to escape loving.

But if she let loving have its way...

The more she thought about it, the more she started to smile. And then to chuckle.

It was crazy. It'd never work. Would it?

It might.

Hamster wriggled down beside her, trying to nose his way under the covers. 'Don't you dare,' she told him. 'You're needed in the living room. Your mistress needs all the hugs she can get, and you're just the Hamster to give them to her.'

And Hugo? How would he take to hugs?

Ridiculous, ridiculous, ridiculous.

But a girl had to try. She reached for her phone.

'Nothing ventured...' she whispered and then she took a deep breath and finished the thought with force. 'Nothing gained. Okay, Hamster, listen in. My parents have spent their lives wanting to do things for me that I've thought unreasonable. In return I'm about to ask them to do something that is the most unreasonable thing I can think of. Watch this space, Hamster. We're about to push the limits of loving to outer space.'

CHAPTER THIRTEEN

CHRISTMAS EVE AND Wombat Valley Hospital was almost full. None of last night's injured were ill enough to require evacuation but each needed care, pain relief and reassurance.

They also needed sympathy; indeed, with the road closure, sympathetic ears were required everywhere. Many of the Valley residents had been expecting guests for Christmas or had intended going elsewhere. Now everyone was stuck.

However, most accepted the situation with resignation. The Valley had been cut off before, by fire or by flood. The population moved into planning mode. Those who'd been expecting guests shared provisions with those who'd been going away, and some of them swapped Christmas plans, so by mid-afternoon it seemed to Hugo that everyone seemed to have planned an alternative.

As the day went on and he heard more and more rearranged plans he felt...

On the outer?

He and Ruby could be included in any Christmas in the Valley—he knew that. He only had to say the word. But the Valley assumed that he and Ruby could have a very merry Christmas with Polly. There'd been offerings of food but no offers of hospitality. The Valley was collectively stunned by Pollyanna Hargreaves and the assumption was that he was a lucky man.

'Make the most of it, Doc,' Joe growled. 'There's mistletoe growing over by the church—you want me to cut you a trailer-load? You could string it up in every room. By Christmas night…hmm. Do you have brandy sauce? I could get my girls to make some for you. Add a bit more brandy, like…'

'Joe…'

'Just saying,' Joe said placidly. 'You gotta enjoy Christmas.'

But how could he enjoy Christmas when Ruby was simply…flattened? Her life had been full of broken promises. She'd almost expected this, he thought, and it broke his heart.

And Polly… How could he spend Christmas not thinking about kissing her?

How to spend Christmas avoiding her?

Polly, however, was almost infuriatingly cheerful. She was wearing another of her amazing dresses—hadn't anyone advised her on appropriate dress for a working doctor? She'd appeared this morning in crimson stilettoes, for heaven's sake, and had only abandoned them when Joe pointed out the age of the hospital linoleum.

'Not that I don't love 'em,' he'd said, looking wistfully at her patent leather beauties. 'They're an artwork all by themselves.'

So the compromise was that a pair of crimson stilettoes brightened up the desk of reception, while Polly padded round the wards in her harlequin dress, her reindeer earrings with flashing lights and a pair of theatre slippers.

There wasn't one disapproving comment. She went from ward to ward, she helped in his routine clinic and, wherever she went, chuckles followed.

She'd offered to take over his morning clinic and, the moment people knew, it was booked out. 'Where's she come from?' a normally dour old farmer demanded as he emerged after consulting her for an allergy he'd had a while but had suddenly deemed urgent this morning. 'No matter. Wherever she came from, let's keep the road blocked. She's a keeper.'

A keeper. Right. As if that was going to happen.

Polly headed back to the house at lunch time. By mid-afternoon there was nothing else to do. It was time for Hugo to go home.

He wasn't looking forward to it.

Ruby had spent the morning at Talia's, but she was home again too. She was sitting on the veranda with Hamster on one side and Polly on the other. She looked despondent and didn't manage a smile as Hugo reached them.

Polly might have cheered the Valley up, but she was having less luck with Ruby. The promise of the beach had held the little girl in thrall for months.

'Hey.' Polly smiled, rising to greet him. 'All finished?'

'I...yes.' He was watching Ruby, thinking how impossible this was. Polly had cheered her up for a while with her laughter and her origami and her crazy flour snow, but that was surface stuff. What really mattered was trust.

Hell, he was giving up so much by being here and he couldn't even get this right. No logic in the world could get through this kid's sense of betrayal.

'So everyone's tucked up for Christmas?' Polly was still smiling, but he thought suddenly her smile seemed a bit nervous.

'Yes.'

'Then...' She took a deep breath. 'Hugo, I know this is an impertinence, and I really hope you don't mind, but I've invited guests for Christmas.'

Guests...?

He thought of all the Valley's oldies. The Valley had its share of lonely people but he'd thought they'd all been catered for. Who'd been left out? Polly was just the sort of woman who brought home strays, he thought. Which particular strays had she chosen?

'For Christmas dinner?' he asked, his mind heading straight to practicalities. 'Polly, our turkey's tiny.' It was the turkey Polly had brought—or rather a turkey breast, cryo-packed, enough for a couple at most.

'Our turkey's rubbish,' she told him. 'A minnow. I gave him to Edith and Harry Banks.'

'You gave away our turkey?'

'It was actually my turkey,' she reminded him. 'I bought it from home when I thought I'd be alone here, but now a bigger one's coming.' She tried to beam but there was uncertainty behind it. 'I... If it's okay with you... It's not too late to call it off, but...'

'But what?' he said and if he sounded goaded he couldn't help it. Ruby was on the sidelines, looking just as confused as he was. He didn't need any more confusion.

This woman had blasted her way into their lives and knocked them both off-kilter, he thought, but then...maybe they'd been off-kilter since Grace died. Maybe their foundations had been blasted away and the force of Polly's enthusiasms was simply making them topple.

That was pretty much how he was feeling now. As if there was no solid ground under his feet.

'My parents...' she said. 'I've invited my parents.'

The ground didn't get any more solid. Confusion, if anything, escalated.

'You don't get on with your parents. Isn't that why you're here?'

'I ran away from home.' She looked down at Ruby and smiled. 'How dumb was that? I didn't figure it out until I saw how much your Uncle Hugo loves you that running away was crazy. And cruel. But it seems too late to run back now, so I thought I'd bring them here.'

'You ran away?' Ruby asked and Polly nodded.

'My mum and dad treat me like a little girl and I was trying to make them see I was a grown-up. But grown-ups don't run away.' She took a deep breath and looked directly at Hugo. 'They stay with those they love.'

'Do you love us?' Ruby asked, still puzzled, and Polly gave a wavery smile.

'I might. I don't know yet. But I do know I love my mum

and dad, so this morning I rang them and invited them for Christmas.'

'Didn't you say they've booked out a Harbour restaurant?' Hugo demanded.

'That's just the thing,' she told him, still trying to keep her smile in place. 'Yes, they've booked out the restaurant. They have fifty of their closest friends coming, but most of those friends have been moving in the same social circles for years so if Mum and Dad aren't there they'll hardly be missed. We were in Monaco last year and our Australian friends seemed to get on fine without us. It's me who they will miss. So I thought...'

'You'd invite them here? I thought...they don't even know you're here.'

'They do now,' she confessed. 'Wow, you should have heard the screech on the phone. And I even had to confess about the snake bite. I figured, seeing I'm referred round here as The Doc the Snake Bit, it'd be about two minutes before they found out.' She sighed. 'But I can handle it. I'll just square my chest, tuck in my tummy and face them down.'

There was a moment's stunned silence. He wanted to smile at the vision of Polly with her chest out and tummy in, but he was too...what? Hornswoggled?

Focus on her parents, he thought, because focusing on Polly was far too discombobulating. Her parents, cancelling their amazing Christmas. The best restaurant in Sydney...

'Won't your parents be paying for the restaurant?'

Polly nodded, and then her smile faded.

'They will, but they won't mind, and that's something I need to talk to you about. My parents are over-the-top generous and also over-the-top extravagant. They have the money behind them to back that up. Hugo, if that's likely to be a thing between us...if you mind...then maybe you'd better say so now.'

What was she saying? There were undercurrents everywhere. The question from Ruby, and Polly's answer, kept reverberating in his head.

Do you love us?

I might. I don't know yet.

And now...

If her parents' wealth was likely to be a problem, say so now? Was she thinking future?

'Polly...'

'Because they're coming and they're bringing Christmas with them,' she said, more urgently now. 'I rang them and said I'd love to have them here, but we have a few specific requirements. So Mum's taken it on as a personal challenge and she's loading the choppers as we speak...'

'Choppers?' he said faintly.

'A truck would be better but if the residents of Wombat Valley insist on destroying all roads, you leave us with no choice. So, are my parents welcome or not?'

'Yes,' he said, even more faintly because there was no choice.

'Great.' She gave him a wobbly smile and then she turned to Ruby. 'Ruby, if you really want—if you really, really want—then my mum and dad can put you and your Uncle Hugo into one of their helicopters and take you to the beach. That'll be fine with me. But can I tell you... My mum and dad organise some of the most exciting Christmases I know. One year I even woke up and there was a snowman in my bedroom.'

'A snowman...' Ruby breathed and Polly grinned.

'I know. Ridiculous. Ruby, I don't know what they'll do this year but I know it'll be a Christmas to remember. And it'll be a family Christmas. It'll be you and your Uncle Hugo, and me and Hamster, and my mum and dad. And presents and lovely things to eat and more presents and Christmas carols and fun. And family. You and your Uncle Hugo can go to the beach after Christmas because I'll stay on until you can, but I'd love you to stay at least until tomorrow. I'd love you to share my Christmas.'

And then there was silence.

The whole world seemed to hold its breath—and Hugo held his breath even more.

The generosity of this woman...

She'd come here to escape. She'd been bruised and battered and bitten and yet she was staying. More, she'd now invited the very people she was running away from.

She was doing this for him, he thought. The helicopters could be an escape for him and for Ruby—or they could mean something more. So much more.

A family Christmas...

'How did they put a snowman in your bedroom?' Ruby sounded as shell-shocked as he was but the fact that she required more information was encouraging.

'It was made with packed ice. We were in Switzerland. Christmas was stormy so we couldn't get out, but that didn't stop Mum getting me the Christmas snowman she'd promised me. It sat in a little paddling pool so it could melt without damaging the hotel's carpet. It had a carrot for a nose and chocolates for eyes and it was wearing my dad's best hat and scarf. Dad got crabby because they got soggy. But there won't be a snowman this year. Mum never repeats herself. There'll be something just as exciting, though. But you don't need to be here, Ruby. You can still have fish and chips on the beach with your Uncle Hugo—if you want.'

And Ruby looked at Hugo. 'What do you want to do?' she whispered and there was only one answer to that.

'I want to stay with Polly.'

'Then so do I,' Ruby whispered and then she smiled, a great beaming smile that almost split her face. 'As long as it's exciting.'

'If Polly's here, I think we can guarantee excitement,' Hugo said gravely, although there was nothing grave about the way he was feeling. He was feeling like a kid in a toyshop—or better. 'Christmas with Polly can't be anything else but excitement plus.'

The Hargreaves senior arrived two hours later, two helicopters flying in low and fast from the east. They landed on the football oval and it seemed half the town came out to see. The Christmas Eve service had just come to an end in the Valley's little church. The locals were wandering home and they stopped to look.

They saw Polly being enveloped.

Polly's mother was out of the chopper before the blades stopped spinning. Olivia was wearing a bright, crimson caftan with gold embroidery. She had Polly's auburn hair—possibly a more vivid version. Her hair was piled in a mass of curls on top of her head, and her huge gold earrings swung crazily as she ran.

Charles Hargreaves was small and dapper and he didn't run, but he still covered the distance to his daughter with speed.

Polly simply disappeared, enveloped in a sandwich hug which looked capable of smothering her.

Hugo and Ruby stood on the sidelines, hand in hand, waiting to see if she'd emerge still breathing.

For Hugo, whose parents had been...restrained, to say the least, this display of affection was stunning.

Ruby's jaw had dropped and was staying dropped. The combination of helicopters, Polly's over-the-top parents and the effusiveness of the greeting left them both awed.

But eventually Polly did break free, wriggling from her parents' combined embrace with a skill that spoke of years of practice. She grabbed a parent by each hand and drew them forward.

'Mum, Dad, this is Dr Denver. And Ruby.'

Charles Hargreaves reached forward to grasp Hugo's hand but Olivia was before him. She surged forward and enveloped him in a hug that matched the one she'd given her daughter.

'You're the dear, dear man who saved our daughter. Snake bite. Snake bite! And us not even knowing. Of all the places... And you saved her. Putting herself at such risk... We knew she shouldn't leave Sydney. Never again, that's what we said, Charles, isn't it? Never again. And what about her blood sugars? What if she'd died out here? I don't know how we can ever...'

Enough. He was enveloped in silk and gold and crimson and he had a feeling if he didn't take a stand now he'd stay enveloped for Christmas. He put his hands on her silk shoulders and put her firmly away from him.

'Mrs Hargreaves, I'm not sure what Polly's told you, but your daughter's made a very good job of saving herself.' He said it strongly, forcibly, because a glance at Polly said that this was important. Her face had sort of...crumpled?

Never again, her mother had said. What sort of strength had it taken to tear herself from these two? But she'd voluntarily brought them back—so he and Ruby could have Christmas.

'Polly's the strongest woman I know,' he continued, and he reached out and took Polly's hand. It seemed natural. It also seemed important and Polly's hand clung to his and he thought: he was right. These two were like bulldozers, and their daughter stood a good chance of being crushed by their force.

'But don't accept my word for it,' he continued. 'The whole Valley agrees. Polly came to this town as the fill-in doctor. She saved two lives the day she arrived. She looks after her own health as well as everyone else's, and she spreads laughter and light wherever she goes. You must have brought her up to be a fiercely independent woman. Her strength is awesome and the whole of Wombat Valley is grateful for it.'

They were taken aback. They stared at him, nonplussed,

and then they stared at Polly. Really stared. As if they were seeing her for the first time?

'She has diabetes,' Olivia faltered and Hugo nodded.

'We have three kids with Type One diabetes in the Valley. Polly's already met one of them. Susy's a rebellious thirteen-year-old and Polly knows just what to say. If Susy can get the same control Polly has, if she can make it an aside to her life as Polly has…well, I'm thinking Susy's parents will be as content and as proud as you must be.'

And it sucked the wind right out of their sails. It seemed they'd come to rescue and protect their daughter, but their daughter was standing hand in hand with Hugo and she was smiling. She had no need of rescue and her armour was re-forming while he watched.

'Polly said…Polly said you might bring a snowman.' Until now, Ruby had been silent. She was on the far side of Hugo, quietly listening. Quietly gathering the courage to speak. 'Polly says you make Christmas exciting.'

And it was exactly the right thing to say. Hugo's arm came around Polly. She leaned into him as her parents shifted focus.

From Polly to Ruby. From Polly to Christmas. He felt Polly sag a little, and he knew it was relief. Somehow energy had been channelled from saving Polly to saving Christmas.

Olivia looked down at the little girl for a long minute, and then she beamed.

'So you're Ruby.'

'Yes,' Ruby said shyly.

'Pollyanna said you wanted to go to the beach for Christmas.'

'We did,' Ruby told her. 'But now… Uncle Hugo and I want to stay with Polly.'

There was a sharp glance at that, a fast reassessment. Hugo expected Polly to tug away, but she didn't. Which was a statement all by itself?

'That's lovely,' Olivia said after a moment's pause. 'Can we stay too?'

'Yes,' Ruby said and smiled and Polly smiled too.

'We have spare bedrooms,' Polly said and Hugo thought *we?*

Better and better.

'Then I guess we need to get these choppers unloaded so the pilots can get back to Sydney for their own Christmas,' Polly's father said, moving into organisational mode. 'Can we organise a truck, Dr Denver?'

'A truck?'

'For the Christmas equipment my wife thought necessary.' Charles gave an apologetic smile. 'My wife never travels light.'

'Excellent,' Polly said and moved to hug her parents. 'Mum, Dad, I love you guys. Ruby, welcome to my parents. My parents are awesome.'

At two in the morning Hugo finally had time to sink onto the veranda steps and assess what had happened over the last few hours.

Polly's parents were overwhelming, overbearing, and they loved Polly to distraction. He could see why she'd run from them. They were generous to the point of absurdity and he could see why she loved them back.

They were also used to servants.

Right now he'd never been more physically exhausted in his life. Polly, on the other hand, didn't seem the least exhausted. She was happily arranging potted palms around a cabana.

There was now a beach where his yard used to be.

The centrepiece was a prefabricated pool it had taken them the night to construct. They'd started the moment Ruby had gone to bed. That had been six hours ago—six hours of sheer physical work. Because it wasn't just a pool. The packaging described it as *A Beach In Your Backyard*, and it was designed to be just that.

A motor came with the pool, with baffles that made waves run from one side to another. Hugo had shovelled a pile of sand—almost a truckload had emerged from the chopper—to lie beside it. A ramp ran up the side—it could be removed to keep the pool child-proof and safe. A lifebuoy hung to the side. Seashells were strewn artistically around. Polly had done the strewing, making him pause to admire her handiwork. There were also sun umbrellas, deckchairs and a tiny palm-covered cabana.

'Because Christmas isn't just for children,' Olivia had decreed as she'd handed over a sheaf of instructions and headed to bed herself. 'There needs to be somewhere to store the makings of martinis. And margaritas. Polly loves margaritas but she's only allowed to have one.'

His eyes had met Polly's at that and laughter had flashed between them, silent but so strong it was like a physical link.

'Don't say a word,' Polly had said direfully and he hadn't.

Charles had helped for the first hour but at the first sign of a blister he, too, had retired. Since then Hugo and Polly had laboured non-stop.

For Ruby's joy was in front of them. In the hope of Ruby's joy he'd even allowed Polly to override his own concerns.

'I want to play Santa as much as you do,' she'd decreed when he'd tried to send her to bed. 'If you fuss, Hugo Denver, I'll throw a tantrum big enough to be heard in Sydney.'

So they'd worked side by side, by torchlight and by the help of a fortuitous full moon. It was hard. It was fun. It was…wonderful.

Six hours of working with Polly was somehow settling things. There were promises being made, unspoken yet—it was much too soon—but working side by side felt right.

It was a promise of things to come? The disintegration of the walls of two different traps?

Whatever it was, now he had a beach in his front garden.

'We've taken over.' Polly had arranged her last palm to her satisfaction. Now she settled onto the step beside him and gazed at the scene before them in satisfaction. 'Goodness, Hugo, are you sure you want us here?'

For answer he reached out and took her grimy and blistered hand. It matched his grimy and blistered hand. He didn't reply. He simply held and the silence settled around them with peace and with love.

They didn't need to say a thing.

'They didn't bring buckets and spades and surfboards,' Hugo said at last, and Polly cracked a guilty grin.

'I checked the back of your wardrobe,' she admitted. 'Hugo, it pains me to admit it but I'm a Christmas snooper from way back. Let me tell you that you're very bad at hiding. The shapes of buckets and spades and surfboards take skill to be hidden and the back of your wardrobe is chicken feed in the hiding stakes.'

'So you told your parents what not to bring?'

'I told them what I thought the bumpy presents were. Mum might be over the top, but she never tries to outshine anyone.'

'Really?'

She giggled. 'Well, she never tries but sometimes she's very, very trying.' She hesitated. 'Hugo, I try not to,' she confessed, 'but I love them.'

'They're hard not to love.'

'You wait until they decide to decorate your bedroom to look like a Manhattan chic hotel…'

'They wouldn't.'

'Only if they love you.' She sighed. 'And they'll probably make you do the painting. Mum'll drink martinis and boss you as you paint. Love doesn't get boundaries.'

'It doesn't, does it?' he said softly and his hold on her hand tightened. 'Polly…'

'Hey, I didn't mean anything by that,' she said hurriedly, as if it was important that she said it. 'I wasn't hinting…'

'You don't need to hint.' He hesitated a moment more, but why not say it? It was all around them anyway.

'Polly, I'm falling in love with you,' he said softly. 'I may have already mentioned it but I'll mention it again now. I have so much baggage I'm practically drowning in it but...'

'By baggage do you mean Ruby?' She sounded incensed.

'I can't leave her.'

'I'd never expect you to. But you think you have baggage! I have Mum and Dad and I've already figured there's no use hiding from them. Wherever I am, they'll be hovering. The term "helicopter parents" takes on a whole new meaning when you're talking about my parents.'

'They love you. They worry.'

'Which infuriates me. It makes me claustrophobic.'

'Are you feeling claustrophobic now?'

'I guess I'm not.' She smiled tentatively. 'You seem to have set new boundaries. They're recalibrating their position but they won't stop worrying.'

'Maybe it's natural.' His hand held hers, gently massaging her fingers. He wanted her so much, and yet he had to say it. There was no space here for anything but truth. 'Polly, I'd worry too.'

She turned and looked at him, square-on. 'When would you worry?'

'If you let me close. As close as I want to be. And Polly, this Valley constricts your life.'

'Like my diabetes.'

'I guess...'

There was another long silence. The night seemed to be holding its breath. There was so much behind the silence, so much it was too soon to say or even think, and yet it was undeniably there.

'If you worried,' she said at last, 'then I might react with anger. I've had enough worry to last me a lifetime.'

'So you might never worry about me?'

He'd been running the hose into the pool. It was now almost full. The moonlight was glimmering on its surface. A wombat had been snuffling in the undergrowth as they worked. Now it made its way stealthily up the ramp and stared at the water in astonishment. It bent its head and tentatively tasted.

'Happy Christmas, Wombat,' Hugo whispered and Polly's hand tightened in his and she smiled.

'It is a happy Christmas. And Hugo, okay, maybe I would worry. Maybe I already do worry. You're a surgeon with amazing skills. You've uprooted yourself, buried yourself...'

'Is this what this is? Burying myself?'

She looked out again, at the pool, at the wombat, at the lights of the little hospital and at the moon hanging low over the valley. 'Maybe not,' she whispered. 'But I would still worry. And you'd have the right to tell me it's none of my business.'

'We're moving forward,' he said gently. 'Into places I hardly dare hope...'

'Me too,' she whispered. 'But maybe we're allowed to hope? Maybe we even have grounds for hoping?'

'Maybe we're stretching our boundaries,' he said softly. 'Figuring they can be stretched. Figuring how to see them as challenges and not chains.'

'I thought I was trapped by family,' she whispered. 'And you're trapped with family too. Maybe the way not to feel trapped is...to combine?'

'Polly...'

'Hush for now,' she whispered. 'Think about it. Just know that I'm thinking about it all the time.'

And it was enough, for now. They sat on, in silence, the stillness of the night enveloping them. It was too soon, too fast, there were too many things ahead of them to even think this could be a beginning, but somehow hope was all around them.

'It's almost full,' Polly ventured at last, almost inconsequentially. 'The pool...'

'That's why I'll stay sitting out here. To turn the hose off.'

'Really? I thought you were sitting because you're too exhausted to move?'

He grinned, and then he kissed her because it seemed okay. No, it seemed more than okay. No touching? *Ha!* Rules were made to be broken. The kiss was long and lingering, insidious in its sweetness and an affirmation of the future all by itself.

And then the first splash of water hit the ground and if a flooded garden was to be avoided they had to pull apart. So Hugo went to turn off the tap while Polly looked at the water, and looked up at the stars and made a decision.

'You should always trial Christmas gifts before the day,' she said as he returned to her. 'What if it's faulty?'

'The wombat already tried it.'

'And then he waddled away. What if he thought there was something wrong? He could hardly have reported it.'

'So you're suggesting...what?'

'A swim,' she said promptly. 'Just to make sure.'

'Me?'

'Both of us. It'd be kind of cool.'

'This water comes straight from the creek. It hasn't had any warmth from the sun yet. You can bet it'll be cool.'

'Chicken.' She rose. 'I'm putting on my bikini.'

'You have a bikini?'

'With polka dots. You want to see?'

'Yes,' he said fervently.

'Only if I get to see you in boxers.'

'How do you know I don't wear budgie smugglers?'

She grinned. 'You're not that type of man. I know it.'

'How do you know?'

'Intuition,' she said happily, heading up the steps to the front door. 'But it's not infallible. Will I still love you if you turn out to be a man who wears budgie smugglers? Watch this space, Dr Denver. In the fullness of time, all will be revealed.'

But he didn't follow. 'Polly, wait.' He hesitated, not because he wanted to, but because things were suddenly moving with a speed that made him dizzy. Boundaries seemed about to be crossed, and if he was to ask Polly to step over them then honesty was required. She needed to see the things he'd railed against for the last twelve months for what they were.

She turned and smiled back at him, but her smile faded as she saw his face. 'What? Are you about to tell me you've two wives and nineteen children in Outer Mongolia?'

'Only Ruby.'

'Then what's the problem?'

'Polly, there's no ER here. We have no specialists on call. There's no three hat restaurant or even a decent curry takeaway. Everyone knows everyone and everyone knows everyone else's business. If you dive into the pool in a polka dot bikini it'll be all over the town by morning.'

'Really?'

'The wombat's reporting it to the grapevine this very minute.'

She didn't smile. 'Do you hate it?' she asked and the question caught him off guard.

Did he hate it?

There'd been times in the past year when he had. There were still times when he longed for his old life, his old job, his friends. But now...

He'd learned to love this little hospital, he thought. Joe and his teasing. Barb and her incessant knitting. Mary and her worries. And his patients... He was becoming part of the lives of the Valley and he was finally starting to see why his father had worked here for so long.

But would he still escape if he could?

Not if Polly was here.

And suddenly he thought that even if she wasn't, things had changed. Polly had brought him laughter. She'd brought smiles to his little niece. She'd brought him Christmas.

But more. She'd brought him courage and, no matter what happened now, something of her would stay.

Did he hate Wombat Valley? Suddenly it was like asking: Did he hate life?

'I did hate it,' he said slowly. 'But I hadn't figured that all it needed was a dusting of polka dots.'

'And flour,' she said and grinned. 'Flour's important. And tatted angels. I'm learning fast. By next Christmas you could have tatted angels from one end of the house to the other.'

'That sounds okay to me,' he said, and it felt okay.

Actually, it felt more than okay. It felt excellent.

'But you?' he asked, because he had to be fair. He had to know. 'Polly, I will not trap you.'

And in answer she walked back down the steps and she took his hands. 'I'm not walking from one trap into another,' she said softly. 'Eyes wide open, I'm stepping into magic.'

Christmas *was* magic, he thought, as finally they broke away and he headed inside for his board shorts. Kiss or not, decision or not, Polly was still insisting on a swim and Polly was bossy and he had the gravest forebodings of bossiness to come.

He couldn't wait.

But for now they were heading for a swim and maybe it wouldn't even be cold.

For magic happened. It was the night before Christmas and the night was full of promise of magic to come.

CHAPTER FOURTEEN

HUGO HAD SLEPT for three hours or maybe a bit less before a squeal broke the stillness of dawn.

Polly had tied a balloon to the end of Ruby's bed, with a red ribbon stretching across the floor and out of the open window. Ruby had obviously found the ribbon.

There was another squeal, longer than the first, and then a yell of pure joy.

'Uncle Hugo! Polly! Hamster! Everyone! Santa's been and he's left a...a pool! There's sand and umbrellas and it's just like the beach. And there's presents piled up beside it and *ohhhhhh...*'

They heard a thud as she jumped out of her window and then hysterical barking as Hamster discovered the enormous intruder in his yard.

'I'd better sneak back to my bedroom before she finds me,' Polly murmured, laughing, and he rolled over and smiled down into her dancing eyes.

'Why would she come and find you when she has a beach?'

'Uncle Hugo!' The yell from outside was imperative. 'Come and see!'

He had to come and see. He had no choice, he thought, as he hauled on his pants and headed for the door, giving Polly time to work out a decorous strategy for her appearance.

He had no choice at all, he thought, as he walked through the front door and was hit by the world's biggest hug from the world's most excited seven-year-old.

'How wonderful!' He emerged from the hug to find that

somehow Polly had made it back to her bedroom and was leaning out of her window, smiling and smiling as she called to them both, 'Happy Christmas, Hugo. Happy Christmas, Ruby. Yay for Santa.'

He had no choice at all, Hugo thought as Ruby dragged him forward to inspect every aspect of this amazing transformation of his yard.

He hadn't had a choice twelve months ago and he didn't have a choice now.

And the strange thing was, no choice at all seemed wonderful.

Polly lay on her sunbed beside the swimming pool and thought about dozing but the world was too big, too wonderful, too full of magic.

Around her was the litter of Christmas. Ruby had woken to little-girl magic, to gifts she loved, to excitement, to fun. She was now asleep on a daybed, cuddled between Olivia and Hamster. Charles was asleep on the next bed.

Weird, wonderful, somehow fitting together...

Family.

She wouldn't run again, Polly decided. She didn't need to.

For Hugo was coming towards her, striding up the slope from the hospital. He'd gone across to check Bert Blyth for chest pain. It'd be indigestion, Polly thought. Hospitals the world over would be filling with indigestion after Christmas dinner.

'All clear?' she asked as he reached her. She stretched languorously, deliciously, and he sat down beside her and tugged her into his arms.

'All done.' He kissed her nose. 'If you stay out in the sun you'll get more freckles.'

'I have cream on.'

'I'm not complaining. I like freckles. Polly, I don't have a gift for you.' He hesitated and then kissed her again, more deeply this time. And when he put her away his smile had faded.

'It's okay,' she told him. 'I don't have a gift for you either.'

'We could take a raincheck until the roads are open. We could buy each other socks. Socks are good.'

'I don't have a lot of time for socks.'

'Really?' He was holding her shoulders, looking down into her eyes. 'Then I have another suggestion.'

'Wh… What?'

'What about a partnership?'

Her eyes never left his face. 'A partnership?'

'Polly, you know the partnership I'm thinking of,' he said, and he smiled, his best doctor-reassuring-patient smile. And it worked a treat. She loved that smile.

'But I know that's too soon,' he told her. 'So I thought… what's not too soon is a professional partnership. Wombat Valley has only one doctor and that leaves me on call twenty-four seven. That's more than enough to keep me busy. The Valley could easily cope with a doctor and a half.'

'A half,' she said dubiously. 'So you're offering…'

'Three-quarters.' He was smiling again but there was anxiety in his smile. He wasn't sure, she thought, but then, neither was she. 'Three-quarters each,' he said softly. 'A medical practice where we have time to care for our patients but we also have time to care for ourselves.'

'If this is about my diabetes…'

'It's nothing to do with your diabetes. It's everything to do with Ruby and Hamster and swimming and enjoying the Valley and making origami frogs and maybe even, in time, making a baby or two…'

'A…what?'

'Given time,' he said hastily. 'If things work out. I don't want to propel things too fast.'

'Babies! That's propelling like anything.'

'I'm sorry,' he said hastily, but he kissed her again, lightly at first and then more deeply, making a liar of himself in the process. 'No propelling,' he repeated as the kiss came to a reluctant end. 'A professional partnership first and then, if things go well...maybe more?'

'Wow,' she breathed. 'Just...wow.'

'What do you think?'

What did she think? 'If we're not propelling...I'd need somewhere to live.'

'So you would. There are a few Valley folk who could be persuaded to take in a boarder. Or,' he suggested, even more tentatively, 'we might be able to split this house. We could put a brick wall or six between us.'

'It wouldn't work.'

'No?'

'Not now I've seen you in boxers.' And without boxers, she thought, and she felt her face colour. She looked up at him and she couldn't help but blush, but she managed to smile and he smiled back.

She loved him so much. How could she love someone so fast?

How could she not?

'So you think it's too soon?' he asked.

Define too soon, she thought. Too soon to love this kind, gentle man who'd given up his world for his little niece? This skilled and caring surgeon who had the capacity to twist her heart?

This gorgeous, sexy man who had the capacity to make her toes curl just by smiling?

Too soon?

She forced herself to look away, around at her parents, at Ruby, at Hamster, then at the little hospital and the valley surrounding them.

Too soon?

'It's Christmas,' she whispered. 'Christmas is magic. Christmas is when you wave a wand and start again, a new beginning, the start of the rest of your life.'

'Isn't that New Year?'

'Maybe it is,' she said as the last lingering doubts dissipated to nothing. She tugged him back into her arms and felt him fold her to him. If home was where the heart was, then home was here. 'So we have New Year to come.'

'What could possibly happen in the New Year that could be better than right now?' he murmured into her hair, and she smiled and smiled.

'Well,' she whispered, 'if we sign for a professional partnership on Christmas Day, what's to stop another type of partnership occurring in the New Year?'

And it did.

EPILOGUE

Christmas, one year on. Dawn...

POLLY STRETCHED LANGUOROUSLY in her enormous bed, and Hugo's arm came out to tug her close. Skin against skin was the best feeling in the world, she decided. She closed her eyes to savour the moment. The dawn chorus would soon wake the house. Ruby and Hamster would burst in at any minute, but for now she could just *be...*

With Hugo.

'Happy Christmas, my love,' he murmured, and she snuggled closer.

'Happy Christmas to you too.' But as his hold tightened and she felt the familiar rush of heat and joy, she tugged back. 'Oi,' she said in warning. 'Ruby and Hamster will arrive at any second.'

'So let me announce number one of my Christmas gifts,' he told her. 'One lock, installed last night. Eight years old is old enough to knock.'

'Really?'

'Really.' His arms tightened and he rolled her above him so she was looking down into his eyes. 'So it's Happy Christmas, my love, for as long as we want.'

'Hooray!'

But the house was stirring. There were thumps and rushing footsteps and then whoops as one small girl spotted what was under the Christmas tree. And then they heard Polly's mum's voice...

'We've hidden a gift for Hamster in the backyard,' Olivia

called. 'Let's go help him find it. We'll give those sleepy-heads a few more minutes' rest.'

'Sleepyheads?' Polly murmured. 'Who's she calling a sleepyhead?'

'That would be you.' And it was true. For the last few weeks Polly had seemed to doze any time she had to herself.

The first trimester often did that. She must have fallen pregnant on the first week of their honeymoon.

It had been...that sort of honeymoon.

'But I'll defend you,' Hugo offered. 'If I can just hold you first...'

And who could resist a bargain like that?

It was good to hold. No, it was truly excellent, Polly decided some time later. She was curved against her husband's body, feeling cat-got-the-cream smug, nowhere near sleep.

Thinking *Christmas*.

Thinking *family*.

How had she ever thought family could be a trap? It had freed them all.

It had even given Hugo back his career.

For two doctors in Wombat Valley had transformed the medical scene. No doctor had wanted to practice here, knowing it meant isolation and overwork. But, with two doctors already committed, more followed.

A couple wanting to escape the rat race of Sydney had looked at Wombat Valley six months ago with fresh eyes. Doctors Meg and Alan Cartwright had bought Doc Farr's vineyard, but the vineyard was a hobby and they needed income to support it.

That meant the Valley now had four doctors, which meant there was cover for holidays. They could go to the beach. What was more, the locals no longer had to go to Sydney for thoracic surgery. A new, stable road meant Hugo could operate twice a week at Willaura. Meg's specialty was urology so she spent a couple of days in Willaura too. The rotation of surgical medical students through Willaura had increased. Hugo could even teach.

It was all Hugo wanted.

No. It wasn't all he wanted.

He wanted Polly and Ruby and Hamster. He even wanted Polly's parents, which was just as well, as Charles and Olivia were constant visitors.

They'd backed off, though. From that first day when Hugo had set the boundaries, they'd accepted them. There was even talk of them building a 'small granny flat', though Polly and Hugo had almost choked when Olivia had explained what she meant by 'small'.

That was for the future, though. For now, for this Christmas, Charles and Olivia were once again staying in their house. 'For how can we not be there on Christmas morning to share the joy?' they'd asked and who could say no? Definitely not Hugo. Definitely not Polly.

For joy was here in abundance. This morning they'd tell them about the baby. They'd already told Ruby. 'It's a secret,' they'd told her, and Ruby was almost bursting with excitement.

'Happy?' Hugo asked. They could hear Olivia and Charles, Hamster and Ruby, heading back to the house. Lock or no lock, their peace was about to be blasted.

'Can you doubt it?'

'I don't doubt it,' he murmured. 'Not for a moment.' He kissed her deeply and then swung out of bed—and paused. Polly's Christmas outfit was hanging by the window, ready for her to slip on. Red and white polka dots. A sash with a huge crimson bow. Crimson stilettoes.

'Wow,' he breathed. 'I thought we'd lost the polka dots for ever.'

'Mum had this made for me,' Polly told him. 'Seeing the snake got the last one.'

'And stilettoes...' He looked at the gorgeous dress with its tiny waist and then he looked at the high stilettoes. He grinned. 'You know, Dr Hargreaves, you may need to consider slightly more staid dressing as our baby grows.'

'Bah! Humbug!' Polly said and chuckled up at him. 'Our baby will love polka dots. Polka dots are delicious, life's delicious and so are you.'

'Package deal?'

'You got it,' she said serenely. 'I have polka dots, life and you, all tied up in one delicious Christmas package. Happy Christmas, Dr Denver. Who could ask for more?'

* * * * *

MILLS & BOON®
Hardback – December 2015

ROMANCE

The Price of His Redemption	Carol Marinelli
Back in the Brazilian's Bed	Susan Stephens
The Innocent's Sinful Craving	Sara Craven
Brunetti's Secret Son	Maya Blake
Talos Claims His Virgin	Michelle Smart
Destined for the Desert King	Kate Walker
Ravensdale's Defiant Captive	Melanie Milburne
Caught in His Gilded World	Lucy Ellis
The Best Man & The Wedding Planner	Teresa Carpenter
Proposal at the Winter Ball	Jessica Gilmore
Bodyguard...to Bridegroom?	Nikki Logan
Christmas Kisses with Her Boss	Nina Milne
Playboy Doc's Mistletoe Kiss	Tina Beckett
Her Doctor's Christmas Proposal	Louisa George
From Christmas to Forever?	Marion Lennox
A Mummy to Make Christmas	Susanne Hampton
Miracle Under the Mistletoe	Jennifer Taylor
His Christmas Bride-to-Be	Abigail Gordon
Lone Star Holiday Proposal	Yvonne Lindsay
A Baby for the Boss	Maureen Child

MILLS & BOON®
Large Print – December 2015

ROMANCE

The Greek Demands His Heir	Lynne Graham
The Sinner's Marriage Redemption	Annie West
His Sicilian Cinderella	Carol Marinelli
Captivated by the Greek	Julia James
The Perfect Cazorla Wife	Michelle Smart
Claimed for His Duty	Tara Pammi
The Marakaios Baby	Kate Hewitt
Return of the Italian Tycoon	Jennifer Faye
His Unforgettable Fiancée	Teresa Carpenter
Hired by the Brooding Billionaire	Kandy Shepherd
A Will, a Wish...a Proposal	Jessica Gilmore

HISTORICAL

Griffin Stone: Duke of Decadence	Carole Mortimer
Rake Most Likely to Thrill	Bronwyn Scott
Under a Desert Moon	Laura Martin
The Bootlegger's Daughter	Lauri Robinson
The Captain's Frozen Dream	Georgie Lee

MEDICAL

Midwife...to Mum!	Sue MacKay
His Best Friend's Baby	Susan Carlisle
Italian Surgeon to the Stars	Melanie Milburne
Her Greek Doctor's Proposal	Robin Gianna
New York Doc to Blushing Bride	Janice Lynn
Still Married to Her Ex!	Lucy Clark

MILLS & BOON®
Hardback – January 2016

ROMANCE

The Queen's New Year Secret	Maisey Yates
Wearing the De Angelis Ring	Cathy Williams
The Cost of the Forbidden	Carol Marinelli
Mistress of His Revenge	Chantelle Shaw
Theseus Discovers His Heir	Michelle Smart
The Marriage He Must Keep	Dani Collins
Awakening the Ravensdale Heiress	Melanie Milburne
New Year at the Boss's Bidding	Rachael Thomas
His Princess of Convenience	Rebecca Winters
Holiday with the Millionaire	Scarlet Wilson
The Husband She'd Never Met	Barbara Hannay
Unlocking Her Boss's Heart	Christy McKellen
A Daddy for Baby Zoe?	Fiona Lowe
A Love Against All Odds	Emily Forbes
Her Playboy's Proposal	Kate Hardy
One Night...with Her Boss	Annie O'Neil
A Mother for His Adopted Son	Lynne Marshall
A Kiss to Change Her Life	Karin Baine
Twin Heirs to His Throne	Olivia Gates
A Baby for the Boss	Maureen Child